Voices Beyond The Creek

by

Curt Richards

Cover Art by *Lea Schizas*

The Wild Rose Press, Inc.
PO Box 708
Adams Basin, NY 14410-0708
Visit us at www.thewildrosepress.com

Publishing History
First Edition, 2025
Trade Paperback Print ISBN 978-1-5092-6324-0
Digital ISBN 978-1-5092-6325-7

Published in the United States of America

Dedication

To my wife, India, who encourages me when I get discouraged. Thank you!

Chapter 1

Smoky's coal-black eyes stared out of their sunken sockets, making Caleb slide to a halt on the gravel parking lot at Fletcher First Baptist Church. He stood frozen with fear as the old battered truck ground into gear and rattled down Cane Creek Road toward the hollow. Just the sight of Smoky Pruitt's stony stare shot waves of terror through Caleb.

As with most small Southern towns in the early 1960s, everyone seemed to know everybody's business. But some folks—like Smoky Pruitt—managed to slip past even the most prying eyes. For Caleb and his friends, Smoky's life in the North Carolina mountains remained a mystery that spawned myths told deep in the night around campfires.

For most of Caleb Austin's fourteen years, he had heard gruesome stories about how Smoky Pruitt hung live animals by their feet in his smokehouses. Tales told about Christmas hams actually being dogs, cured slowly in the rickety old shacks down in the hollow, sent chill bumps dancing across Caleb's skin.

"Young Caleb! Are you going to help me or leave me in the back of this car 'til Jesus comes back?" Miss Whitmire popped him on the leg with her cane, snatching his attention away from Smoky's truck fading down the road into the Sunday morning mist. Caleb rolled his eyes and shook his head as he bent down to help the elderly lady struggle from the back seat of her car. Her tiny hand clutched Caleb's arm while the other hand gripped a wooden cane.

"One day, young man, you're goin' to be needin' some help, too, you know."

Caleb gritted his teeth and forced a cordial "Yes, Ma'am" as Miss Whitmire turned to speak to her driver.

"Now, Alexander, you be back here at noon sharp." For emphasis, she raised her cane slightly and jabbed it toward the black man. Alexander tipped his hat politely and drove the shiny car out of the parking lot toward the colored church across the railroad tracks.

Each Sunday morning, the fourteen-year-old boys' Sunday School class took turns helping Miss Whitmire into the sanctuary. Today had been Bobby Henderson's turn to help, but a few fake sneezes made the Sunday School teacher pick Caleb since he didn't want to give a cold to the oldest member of the church.

However, today wasn't the best Sunday for Caleb to have the dreaded "Whitmire Duty." Marlee, his best friend in the whole world, was being baptized in just a few minutes.

There was no way he was going to miss that.

He nudged Miss Whitmire onto the sidewalk just as Bobby and his band of cronies strolled by.

"Going to the dance, Caleb?" Bobby snickered under his breath before bursting into laughter as the group bounded up the church steps.

That blond-headed snot! Caleb thought. He glared at the back of Bobby's blond head before it disappeared into the sanctuary.

Caleb didn't care if Bobby was from one of the richest families in the county. He wanted to drag him out of the church, baptize him in Cane Creek, and dunk him from his neatly combed hair to his shiny penny loafers.

Caleb snarled but did not comment, just in case Miss Whitmire was listening. But she was wrapped up in her constant drivel about one of her grandsons in the Navy.

The warm September breeze drifted past Caleb and through the open front doors of the church, meeting the organ music as it spilled out onto the concrete porch. By the time they reached the top step, he could hear Preacher Anders making his opening comments from the baptistery. Caleb almost lifted Miss Whitmire's frail body off the floor to tote her piggyback down the aisle and dump her in her special, reserved chair.

Instead, he patiently escorted her into the church, politely waited while she fumbled with her purse, and discreetly handed him the usual prize—one piece of Double Bubble gum. He mumbled thanks, turned, and scurried to his family's pew just as the preacher took Marlee by the hand.

"Upon your public profession of faith in Jesus Christ, and in obedience to his divine command, I now baptize you, Mary Lee Patterson, in the name of the Father, the Son, and the Holy Spirit. Amen."

"What?" Caleb whispered, louder than intended. He stared with disbelief into the baptistery. His Dad lifted one eyebrow and gave his head a slight shake. Caleb got the message and sat quietly.

In Caleb's short life, he had encountered many expected standards of conduct. The sacred worship of God, family loyalties, and the use of corn to catch trout were some unshaken aspects of this mountain culture. Questioning or disobeying an adult was a sure way to get a whippin', or at the very least, wind up raking out the chicken coop—if they had one.

Still, questions raced through his mind as his eyes narrowed and followed Mary Lee out of the sunken metal tub above the pulpit. A thin veil of water washed across her face and down her white gown and dripped onto her bare feet. Still holding the Reverend's hand, she carefully stepped up the wooden stairs where her mother waited with a towel.

The preacher's wrong, thought Caleb as he stood with the rest of the congregation and reached for the tattered hymnal. After all, this was only Preacher Anders's second Sunday. Even Grandpa commented that he had looked greener than a frog's butt. Caleb grinned as he fumbled with the songbook, remembering how his grandma had thumped Grandpa's head for making such a crude comparison.

Marlee and Caleb had known one another as far back as either of them could remember. Whenever Caleb asked his mother how long he and Marlee had been friends, she would raise her hands to the sky and proclaim, "In the beginning, there was Caleb and Marlee," as if she were quoting scripture. This amazed Caleb. Having such a good friend for over fourteen years was literally a lifetime. But this astonishment could not compare to the discovery he made today. Marlee, his lifelong friend, catcher of tadpoles, and climber of trees, was really Mary Lee?

****

It was the last Sunday in September, and it was still warm, especially in the North Carolina mountains. All week the weather seemed to be the main topic of conversation at church and Harper's Store, but at the Sunday dinner table, Caleb had plenty of questions.

None of them were about the weather.

"It just don't make sense." Caleb held a spoonful of mashed potatoes halfway between his mouth and the plate. "I mean, why haven't I ever heard Marlee's real name before? We've never kept secrets."

"Oh, I'm sure you have; you just don't remember. Now that I think about it, they haven't used the name Mary Lee since she left the cradle," Caleb's mother said.

"Old Preacher Taylor knew all our names."

"That's Reverend Taylor, Caleb," his dad corrected, raising an eyebrow once again.

Caleb's mother reached for the bowl of black-eyed peas. "Reverend Anders is still learning. After all, he's the youngest preacher Fletcher First Baptist has ever had, but he sure seems to know the Bible."

"Ol'—I mean Reverend Taylor didn't use so many big words," Caleb said. He reached across his mother's plate toward the mound of fried chicken but was stopped cold by her stare. She picked up the platter of fried chicken and passed it to Caleb.

"Reverend Anders seems like a fine man, but I agree with Caleb. Too many fifty-cent words are tossed around. *Pontificate*. Why the heck doesn't he just say he's going to preach at us? I feel like I need a dictionary and a Bible." Caleb's dad chuckled.

"Well, Joshua, it might do us all some good to stretch our minds a little. You know, not that many people in Fletcher went to college. A lot of folks never even finished grammar school. Having a little education around here will be a good thing."

"Yeah! I saw ol' Smoky Pruitt this morning when I was helpin' Ol' I mean, Miss Whitmire. That man spooks me."

"That's a perfect example of why you need an education. No one wants to wind up in a shack down in the hollow having to smoke hams for a living," Caleb's mother said.

"I'm gonna be an astronaut, so I guess I'll be going to college."

"You doggone right you will." Caleb's dad pointed his fork at his son. "I don't care if you go to college for basket weaving, but you're gonna go. That's the only way you young folks are gonna make it."

"I'm going to make it to the moon, just like President Kennedy said." Caleb slowly lifted his butter knife like a rocket launched from Cape Canaveral.

At that, his mother got up, tied the gingham apron Caleb had given her last Mother's Day around her waist, stacked a few plates, and turned on the hot water faucet in the sink. "If we plan to make it to the Pattersons', we best be moving along."

Caleb changed from his Sunday suit to his Wranglers and favorite sneakers and was waiting on the front lawn, skipping gravel down the asphalt road. This was the last ice cream churn of the year, and Marlee's mother and father had invited them along with the new preacher and his wife to celebrate Marlee's baptism.

Caleb stuck his head out of their new 1961 Buick when it turned into the Pattersons' gravel driveway. It hadn't come to a complete stop before he jerked open the back seat door.

"Don't slam the—" The door banged shut.

Caleb's mother shook her head but smiled as she stepped out of the car. "Caleb, take this into the Pattersons' kitchen for me." She handed her son a basket with two of her award-winning apple pies. Just a week ago Saturday, she had taken home a blue ribbon from the Henderson County Fair for her apple pie recipe. Caleb wanted to hang the ribbon on the mantel, but she put it in the pantry on top of the others she had won in past years. "Doing a good job is reward enough," she had told Caleb.

Marvin Patterson walked toward the car as Caleb rushed past him, carrying the basket to the kitchen.

"Boy, if I could bottle and sell that energy, I'd close my bakery for sure." He stuck his hand out to Caleb's dad, who was rubbing a spot on the hood of the car with his handkerchief. Both men stood, wearing dark blue suits and white shirts, admiring the Buick.

Across the yard, Marlee's sixteen-year-old brother Henry straddled an oak stump while he lazily cranked the ice cream churn.

"Need me to stand on the churn?" Caleb asked.

"Sure, kid, grab a hold of the limb up there."

Caleb carefully stepped onto the top of the churn and held on to the lower limb of the water oak tree.

"Can I crank some?" Caleb asked.

"You're doin' just fine holdin' the churn still for me. Besides, you know what happens if you crank the wrong way, don't ya?" Henry cut his eyes up at Caleb.

"No, what happens?" Caleb strained to turn his head around and look down at Henry, huddled over the churn.

"It'll all turn back into milk and sugar and stuff, and you can never use it for ice cream again. You might as well go ahead and feed it to the dogs then."

"Really? Well, I can do it right."

Caleb balanced on top of the churn and smiled at Marlee, who lay several feet away on the grass, studying the clouds. She sighed heavily and rolled her eyes.

"Henry's just pulling your leg."

"No, I ain't! You just go ask Daddy." Henry turned his head toward the two men standing by the car. "Hey, Daddy! Don't it matter which way you crank the churn?"

The men were deep in discussion. Marlee's Dad glanced at Henry, lit a cigarette, and continued talking. He stood six feet two inches and weighed over two hundred and fifty pounds, but his body parts didn't seem to match. His clothes were roughly tossed about on his large frame, with his ample belly sticking out from beneath his unbuttoned coat. Standing swayback, he appeared to be able to turn and look completely behind him while his feet remained firmly in place.

Caleb's dad was just as tall and thin as all the Austin men. His fine-chiseled features and dark complexion betrayed his Cherokee bloodline. He sported a thick head of black hair, combed back neatly and kept in place by hair tonic. Caleb had been told that he resembled his father as a teenager.

The two women stepped off the porch, carrying a heavy tray of lemonade and ice cream bowls. Marlee's mother glanced at the sky and observed the wispy horsetail clouds. "I do believe that the cold is on its way."

"We just had the harvest moon, so it should be getting chilly soon," Caleb's mother added.

"Ain't that right, Mama?" Henry demanded. "You have to crank the churn one way, or it'll all go back like it was before."

"What kind of story are you tellin' those kids now, Henry? Last summer, you told them some creek story, and all they wanted to do was run off to Cane Creek."

Caleb's mother arranged the ice cream bowls on the picnic table. "From what I hear from Preacher Anders, our young folks could be doing a whole lot worse. Last week, he came and spoke to our circle meeting and told us some of the things going on in Asheville. I just don't know what's gotten into some young folks these days."

"What kind of things?" Caleb turned his head, almost losing his footing on the churn.

"For one, he told us about his old church being broken into and things stolen."

"My stars! Someone stealin' from a church? You just can't get any worse than that, you know?" exclaimed Marlee's mother.

"Yeah, he told us the same story in Sunday School. They never caught 'em, so how does he know it was young folks?" offered Henry as he jerked the churn handle hard.

Mrs. Patterson stopped setting the cups out and peered over her glasses at her son. Henry quickly returned his attention to churning the ice cream. Marlee sat up on one elbow. "We had someone steal from our church."

"When?" asked her mother.

"Last Christmas."

"Oh, you're not talking about that dumb old doll of yours?" Henry groaned.

"It's not a dumb doll; it was the baby Jesus!" Marlee jumped and stuck her hands on her hips.

"It was an old ratty doll of yours. Besides, you didn't want it anyhow."

"Did too! I loved that doll!"

"Yeah, yeah." Henry gave the churn a few forceful cranks.

"You know," Caleb's mother broke in, "it was strange how that doll disappeared and then showed up on

Christmas morning."

"It just made me wonder what kind of person would steal a doll out of a manger anyhow," Mrs. Patterson said. "I mean, what's this world comin' to? It's not like we live in Asheville. This is Fletcher, for gosh sakes!" She turned and headed for the house. "I'm goin' to look in on your apple pies. I'll be right back."

With a few more minutes of hard cranking and Caleb holding tight to the water oak limb, the ice cream was ready. Preacher Anders and his wife arrived and said their hellos. The adults relaxed in lawn chairs under the tree, enjoying ice cream and pie and, of course, discussing the weather.

Henry retreated to the large porch that wrapped halfway around the Pattersons' house. He stretched out his large frame comfortably in a rocker and rested his feet on the banister. He looked relaxed, eating his ice cream and reading a Superman comic, when Caleb and Marlee came to the porch.

"Why don't y'all go sit somewheres else."

"Free country!" Marlee barked.

"Hey, I've got some important readin' to do here."

Marlee grabbed her ice cream bowl and stormed down the steps. "Come on, Caleb, I told you he wouldn't want to talk about it."

"Talk about what?" Henry laid the comic in his lap as he took a large spoonful of ice cream.

"I wanted to hear more about the creek people," Caleb said.

"What do you want to know? You want to know how they hear the voices in the creek? Or that ol' Smoky Pruitt actually smokes dogs he steals instead of hams!" Henry leaned toward Caleb and Marlee and let out a low, scary laugh.

"I did hear that he went crazy after his wife died," Caleb added.

"Died? Is that what you think happened?" He produced a large smirk and sat back in his rocker.

"Well, that's what my mama said."

"They don't know what happened. Gerald Martin told me all about it." Henry leaned forward again and rested his elbows on his knees. He slowly twisted his neck over his shoulder like he was ready to reveal a very important secret. With a hushed voice, he continued. "My buddy, Gerald, was huntin' on the other side of Cane Creek one day, and he saw ol' Smoky tote her into one of his smokehouses."

"Gosh! No foolin'?" Caleb's eyes were as wide as the ice cream bowl balancing on Henry's knee.

Marlee elbowed Caleb. "Course not, Caleb. Henry and dumb Gerald just sit around makin' up this stuff to try and scare us."

"Well, then, why does that Pruitt girl run around barefoot wearing a burlap seed sack for a dress?" Henry asked. "It's what that 'shine will do to you. They say ol' Smoky mixed up a bad batch, went crazy and killed his wife, then stuffed her in one of his smokehouses. That li'l girl went plum crazy after that, too. 'Course, I don't think she had far to go as it was."

"She's not crazy, she's just...retarded, or somethin'," Marlee said.

"Retarded?" Henry countered. "Spooky is what she is. Seems like I remember somethin' about them knowin' she was different from the day she was born. She even lives in the smokehouse with her smoked mama."

Caleb gulped a deep breath and held it.

Curt Richards

"The longer you sit here, the bigger his story gets," Marlee warned.

"I'm tellin' the truth! She's in that smokehouse. Maybe you can see her this Christmas when you go down in the hollow to get the church hams!" Henry threw his head back and let loose a howl of laughter so hard that his rocker tilted backward, making him lose his balance. The Superman comic book went sailing, and the melted vanilla ice cream spilled down the front of his shirt. Arms and legs flew in the air.

This whole spectacle reminded Caleb of the time he threw a stray cat high in the air to see if it would land on its feet. It did.

And so did Henry. His feet came down onto the wooden porch with a loud thud, followed by an even louder string of words that would surely make the men down at the sawmill blush.

The kids immediately jerked their heads toward the group of adults sitting around the water oak tree.

Mr. Patterson was already marching towards the porch, his face red as an orchard apple. Henry responded in the only manner fitting a sixteen-year-old boy who had just cussed in front of his parents, his neighbors, and the preacher. He grabbed his ankle and fell to the floor, writhing in false torment.

"You better have a good reason, boy, or I'll give you something to holler about!"

Caleb and Marlee left their ice cream on the steps and headed in the direction of Cane Creek. Both of them had learned long ago that when an adult was angry, it was possible to receive punishment by simply being present.

****

12

The well-worn path was now covered with fallen leaves that crunched as they walked beside the creek. The leaves from the poplar tree floated like yellow mats, gaining speed and breaking apart as they traveled across the rapids. The debris covered the tiny pool where Caleb and Marlee caught tadpoles last summer. Marlee slipped her shoes off and walked barefoot down the bank, balancing herself by holding on to the skinny trunk of a sourwood tree. Caleb stood on the bank and watched Marlee's graceful movements as she stopped, picked up a stick, and slowly stirred the leaves floating in the pool.

Caleb stepped out on nearby Turtle Rock and sat on the cool granite boulder. When Caleb and Marlee first spotted the rock a few summers back, they decided the outcrop looked like the head of a snapping turtle. Ever since, they had always called their favorite place Turtle Rock.

"No tadpoles," Marlee said, still stirring the water.

"Nope, not with cooler weather comin' soon," Caleb answered.

"I wonder where the frogs that we raised this summer went. We let 'em go right over there." Marlee tossed her stick in a deep area under the rock outcropping where Caleb was sitting.

"Summer sure was fun," Caleb said, a sad tone to his voice. He flipped an acorn into the creek and watched as it floated out of sight.

"There's always Thanksgiving," Marlee said.

"That's two months away. Maybe it'll snow before then, and we'll get a day off from school!"

"School hasn't started but about a month, and you already want days off. Caleb, I swear, you sound more like Henry every day."

Caleb turned to Marlee and smiled. "I wish I was in your class. Y'all seem to always be doin' somethin' fun."

"Mrs. Douglass is a fun teacher. She told us that this Halloween, we're going to have a pumpkin carving contest!"

"Ol' Miss Simms wouldn't let us do anythin' fun like that. All we do is work and collect canned goods."

"Y'all already startin' that? Usually, they don't do the food drive 'til close to Thanksgiving."

"You should see her desk. She has ribbons taped all around it. She always wins the paper drive and canned food drive. I think if we don't win this year, she'll fail us all!"

"Hey, then you'd better get on down to Harper's and buy some beans! I can't go on up to high school next year and leave you behind!" Marlee teased.

For a while, they sat, tossing acorns into the creek and watching an occasional leaf wind its way through the branches and fall into the water. Marlee's brow was furrowed while she twisted a blonde curl around her finger. "You know, I'm glad I'm not poor and have to take stuff from people I don't know. What if your only Thanksgiving food was canned beans and, for Christmas, some old hand-me-down toy?"

"I don't have a brother or sister to get or give anythin' to. Hey, maybe you can wear Henry's old clothes!" Caleb teased.

"No way! I'd rather run around neckked!

Caleb blushed.

Marlee laughed and punched Caleb on the shoulder. "Come on, let's head back before Henry gets all the apple pie." Marlee stood up, brushed off her dress, and slipped on her shoes.

When they turned toward the trail, Caleb grabbed Marlee by the arm. "Shhhhh," he ordered, staring across the creek. "I hear somethin'." He pointed into a thicket, just a short distance up the creek but on the opposite side.

"Maybe it's the creek talking."

"No, this was somethin' in the bushes."

Last year, Henry told them that the creek voices would tell someone where the fish were biting if they listened hard enough. This was how the creek people who lived in the shacks down in the hollow got their food. But he also claimed that sometimes, if you listen closely enough, the creek would warn you of impending doom.

With Henry's stories of Smoky Pruitt fresh in his mind, Caleb turned and scurried up the trail in front of Marlee. He peered over his shoulder at the brush across the creek. "Let's get on back home."

"I don't hear...wait a minute. Someone *is* there." Marlee bent over and put her hands on her knees.

"C'mon, let's get outta here."

"Look! I can see somebody over there." Marlee ignored Caleb's plea and craned her neck, peering across the creek.

"Marlee, leave it be. Let's go...you know...apple pie?" He ran back and tugged at her arm.

Suddenly, the figure across the creek jumped up and looked at them. It was a girl, about nine or ten years old. She wore an old, ragged dress and high-topped leather shoes with no laces. Her hair flopped across her face, so they almost didn't recognize her.

"That's Annabelle Pruitt," Marlee whispered.

"You mean, one of the—"

"Hi, Annabelle!" Marlee waved across the creek.

The girl stood still and stared. It was difficult to tell if she heard or understood Marlee's words. Without warning, she disappeared through the brush.

Chapter 2

Marlee hurried to the edge of the creek and stopped before her shoes touched the water. Any other time, Caleb knew that she wouldn't have hesitated to splash through the creek, but if she came home with wet shoes and a muddy dress today, her mother would have a few good words for her, to say the least.

"Hello!" Marlee called into the doghobble thicket on the opposite bank. Caleb stood, sheltered by a poplar tree, and watched, expecting Smoky Pruitt and his hounds to come crashing through the brush any minute.

"Annabelle. Are you there?" Marlee bent and studied the undergrowth. Suddenly, Annabelle appeared next to a large hickory tree. The girl stood motionless, like a rabbit spotted in a briar thicket. Her hair was shoulder-length and unkempt, and she wore a dirty dress that draped to mid-calf, ending a few inches above her leather shoes.

Caleb peeked out from behind the poplar tree and watched Annabelle stare at Marlee with piercing blue eyes. They weren't the dull, somber eyes of the kids at school who made up the small Yellow Bird reading group. There was sadness, and yet an intelligent awareness in her eyes. Caleb heard Henry's words in his brain: "She was different from the day she was born."

Annabelle slipped back into the thicket and was gone as quickly as she had appeared.

****

The trail followed a gentle slope along Cane Creek before turning towards Thompson's meadow and emptied into the Patterson's property. Caleb walked ahead, hitting newly fallen leaves with a stick he had picked up beside the creek.

Caleb could tell that Marlee was lost in thought, wrestling with something. He didn't ask. She looked at the ground as she walked and twisted a lock of her hair tightly around her finger. When Caleb's mama would ask his daddy what he was thinking about, he would run his fingers through his hair and reply, "I just have something to chew on for a bit." Then, she would leave him alone. Now, Caleb left Marlee to her thoughts.

The two strolled silently along the path underneath a blaze of hickory and poplar trees that blanketed the ground with their yellow leaf litter. Caleb liked that he could be with Marlee without having to talk. Eventually, Marlee turned to Caleb and broke the silence.

"Why do you think she took off like that? We weren't going to do anything to her. She didn't need to be afraid of us."

Caleb shrugged.

"Why doesn't Annabelle go to our school?" Marlee asked.

"I don't think she goes to school anywhere. One time, Mama said that a special teacher was going out to her place. Seems like I remember when we were in the fourth or maybe fifth grade, she was in the first. But then I heard that her mama died."

Marlee's eyes widened. "Yeah, that's right! Come to think of it, I never saw her after that. At school anyways."

****

When they arrived at the edge of the Patterson's property, Caleb tossed his stick into the brush and turned to Marlee. "Why you thinkin' so much about Annabelle Pruitt?

"Seeing her in person got me thinking. You know I love a good mystery."

Caleb knew this to be true. Last summer, it seemed like all that Marlee wanted to do was sit by Cane Creek and listen to the sounds that gurgled from the water flowing over the rocks. Marlee swore that she had heard voices.

"But it also hurts my heart to think about how she has to live, you know, in that old smokehouse," Marlee continued.

"So you believin' some of the stories Henry was tellin'?" Caleb asked.

"Course not! I just like to help people. I guess that's why I want to be a nurse when I grow up. I was thinking that maybe we could help Annabelle somehow."

"*We*?" Caleb's eyes widened.

"Well, not right now, anyway." Marlee stepped in front of Caleb and started running toward the house. "Race ya for the apple pie!"

Caleb ran behind her. He was thin as a twig, a fast runner, but Marlee was a head taller and had longer legs. She easily beat him to the porch, where they collapsed in the swing, laughing, out of breath.

"There you two are." Mrs. Patterson opened the screen door to the kitchen, drying her hands on her striped apron as she spoke. "We've got apple pie, and there's still some ice cream left. C'mon and get some."

****

The kitchen was bright with its white cabinets and light green linoleum floor. Several framed prints of teapots hung on the daffodil wallpaper. Caleb's mother sat at the kitchen table and sipped coffee.

Caleb and Marlee stood by the counter and watched as Mrs. Patterson cut two wide pieces of homemade apple pie. She then scooped from the churn a hill of vanilla ice cream. The pie was still warm, and the ice cream began to melt in little white puddles around the golden pie crust.

"Caleb, the men folk are in the den watching the ball game. You can take your pie in there if you want to," Mrs. Patterson said.

Caleb walked through the doorway into the living room, carefully balancing his plate of pie so that none spilled. He wanted to be with the men, but he didn't care much for watching football. He also wanted to be with Marlee, so he sat on the edge of the rug just outside the kitchen to eat his pie and ice cream, occasionally glancing up at the TV but intent on the conversation in the kitchen. From where he sat, Caleb could see Marlee sitting at the table with his mother.

"Margaret, come sit down for a bit and have some coffee. Those men can clean up after themselves. You're making me nervous." Caleb's mother chuckled as Marlee's mother hurried back into the kitchen with an empty pie plate.

"So, Marlee, what have y'all been up to?" Her mother scooped up a couple of plates and set them in the sink.

"We saw Annabelle today."

"Well, okay, just let me rinse these plates 'fore they get all—" Mrs. Patterson looked back over her shoulder at Marlee. "Annabelle? You mean Annabelle Pruitt?"

"Yep. Caleb and me went—"

"Caleb and *I*," her mother corrected, reaching for the dishwashing detergent.

"Well, we both saw her down at Turtle Rock this afternoon."

"What was she doing this far up the creek?" Caleb's mother asked. She stirred a dollop of cream into her coffee.

"I don't know. We were about to leave when I looked across the creek and saw her peeking through the brush at us."

"Did she say anything?"

"No. When I said hello, she just turned and ran."

"I didn't even know the child could talk." Mrs. Patterson poured more coffee into Caleb's mother's cup before refilling her own. "A child like that surely needs to be watched after. It's just not proper, her runnin' around wild. What was it I heard some years back 'bout her bein' retarded?"

"No, she's not retarded or anything of the sort." Caleb's mother shook her head. "She went to school through the first grade and was doing fine from what I heard, but then Smoky took her out."

"Why didn't he want her to go to school?" Marlee asked.

"Now, what was it I heard about her? Somethin' about when she was born," Marlee's mother said.

"You know Mattie, who helps Grandma Austin?" Caleb's mother asked.

"Oh, the sweet colored lady. She's been with them for a long time. How many years now?"

"Let's see, Caleb was a toddler when she started,

and he's fourteen now."

"Oh, so she's been there at least a dozen years, don't ya think?"

Marlee looked into the living room and rolled her eyes at Caleb. He saw her knee begin to bounce up and down the way it always did when she got impatient. To him, it seemed that adults changed the subject about as often as the weather changed. Getting in on a conversation between their mothers was like trying to jump on a moving merry-go-round.

Caleb rolled his eyes at Marlee, and she returned a cross-eyed gaze. Laughing, he almost spit out a mouthful of pie.

"So, why didn't Annabelle stay in school?" Marlee attempted to get the discussion back on track.

Caleb's mother took another sip of coffee. "You see, Mattie used to midwife some, and she helped deliver Annabelle. She said that Annabelle was born with the veil."

"That's right!" Marlee's mother snapped her fingers. "I knew I remembered somethin' different 'bout that child."

"A veil?" Marlee asked. "Like a wedding veil?"

Marlee's mother leaned toward her daughter and wrinkled her brow. "Well…" she glanced into the next room. Caleb fixed his eyes on the TV, but he was tuned into the kitchen conversation, especially since the voices now took on hushed tones.

"It's the birth sac. Some babies are born with it over their faces, so they call it a veil. It kinda makes them different."

"Different? How?" Marlee leaned across the table, intrigued.

"Some can see the future or even see spirits and such."

"But those stories are nothin' but old wives' tales," Caleb's mother said.

"That's true, but then, I'm an old wife!"

The two mothers laughed.

"Why're you so interested in Annabelle Pruitt all of a sudden?" Marlee's mother wiped under her coffee cup with a napkin.

"There was just something about her. When she looked at me, it was like she…" Marlee stopped and wrinkled her brow.

"Like she what?"

"Kinda like she knew something, and…well…that I didn't."

"Oh, she just knows she's different 'cause she's poor and lives down in the hollow. She's probably embarrassed. All her daddy does is sell smoked hams, and some folks say he makes liquor, too." Marlee's mother sat straight up in her chair, eyebrows raised. "But I wouldn't know about that. I don't take to gossipin', you know."

"He must get it somewhere. I've only been around the man a couple of times, but he smelled like he used it for aftershave!" Caleb's mother chuckled. Both ladies laughed.

"I know they're poor, but there's just something else," Marlee said quietly.

"You know ol' Smoky could work and do better. Matter of fact, they say he was a pretty good house painter before his wife died." Marlee's mother stood up and took Marlee's empty plate to the sink. "But now I guess he just does as he pleases."

"I reckon so, but that's sad for that li'l girl, especially at this time of year. Our Sunday School class tried to take another care package to them last Christmas. Remember when we went to get the hams for the church?" Caleb's mother asked.

Marlee's mother turned around and dried her hands on her apron. "I remember that. He wouldn't even take a stick of candy for that little girl. Broke my heart. That's what it did, broke my heart."

"What was it like at Annabelle's house?" Marlee turned towards Caleb's mother.

"Well, it was unkempt, for starters. Everything was dirty and junky. And the poor girl's clothes were ragged as well. We came back the very next day and brought some things that people had donated, but I don't know if she ever got them."

"Why not? Didn't y'all give them to her?" Marlee asked.

"Oh, we tried. We tried to give them to her daddy, but he told us to set them on the porch. Then he made some comment about not needing anybody's charity."

"Pride. Such a sinful thing…" Marlee's mother stopped. "You know, didn't Annabelle's mother have *two* children? Seems I heard that somewhere."

"I don't really recall; I know her mother got sick while carrying another child."

Marlee set her milk glass down on the table with a loud thud. "You mean she has a sister or a brother?"

"All I know is that she was expecting. People say she had the baby and then got sick. No one helped with the birth. Not that I know of anyways," Caleb's mother explained.

Marlee's mother leaned slightly across the table and

looked back over her shoulder toward the den. "Some folks say he killed 'em both," she said with a whisper.

"And put them in the smokehouse! Oh, Mama, you sound just like Henry now!" Marlee laughed.

****

Soon, it was halftime, and the men went to the porch for a smoke. Henry positioned himself in front of the TV and began switching between the two channels, looking for another game to watch. But Caleb joined the ladies in the kitchen, hoping for a second helping of apple pie.

"Annabelle might have a brother or a sister!" Marlee said.

Caleb shrugged, pretending that he hadn't heard them talking. "So?"

Caleb's mother stared out of the window. She seemed to be deep in thought. "You know, now that I think about it, I think I remember some talk down at the Social Services."

"What talk?" Marlee said.

"It seems that Mr. Pruitt was applying for government aid and claimed that he had two children. Another girl, I believe."

"So, Annabelle *does* have a sister?"

"According to Mr. Pruitt. He said she never was in her right mind and that she lives with his wife's sister up in Hickory, I believe he said." She turned the cup in her hands and wrinkled her brow. "She should be about four or so."

"If she even exists," Marlee's mother added.

"Why would someone lie about having another kid?" Marlee asked.

"People will do all sorts of things for money," Marlee's mother answered, pointing her finger for emphasis.

"Caleb, how 'bout another piece of pie?"

"Okay." Caleb slid his plate across the table to Mrs. Patterson.

His mother straightened in her chair and squinted her eyes. "You go get that plate right now, young man, and say thank you."

"Uh, yes, Ma'am." Caleb reached for the plate. "Thank you, Mrs. Patterson."

"Why, you are certainly welcome." Mrs. Patterson smiled at Caleb as she leveled a heaping slice of pie onto his plate.

The screen door slammed as the men came back inside and took their places in the den.

"C'mon, Caleb, bring your pie out to the porch," Marlee said.

"Stay in the yard now, Caleb. We're going before long." His mother's voice followed him out the door.

But Caleb knew that when the parents began to talk about leaving, they had about thirty minutes before the car doors were opened and about ten more minutes before the car pulled out of the driveway.

On the porch, Marlee marched back and forth across the wooden floorboards and occasionally paused at the banister like some speech-making politician. Caleb watched for a few minutes as he finished the last bites of his pie. It was true that Marlee loved to solve a mystery. The only time that Caleb could remember her being scolded at school was when she hid a novel behind her geography book. When the teacher asked her what was the capital of Portugal, she blurted out, "Nancy Drew!"

What was so special about this Pruitt girl, anyhow? Caleb didn't think that Annabelle was *that* mysterious.

She was just another poor kid from the hollow.

But he listened. After all, Marlee was his friend, and that's what friends do.

Chapter 3

The night was perfect. If Caleb had painted a picture of Halloween, it would have been this night. The hunter's moon was picking itself up off the horizon, turning the black sky into royal blue. Naked oak and hickory limbs cast animated shadows of bony hands across fence lines, and large bales of hay rose from the dark fields like giant tombstones.

Nearly four weeks had passed since they had churned ice cream at Marlee's house. With history reports, science projects, and math problems eating away at his time, Caleb had only seen Marlee when they walked to and from school and for a brief time in church. But tonight, they would forget about school and enjoy their last time trick-or-treating. Caleb and Marlee's parents had told them that when they turned fifteen, there would be no more knocking on neighbors' doors and asking for candy. This last Halloween was to be a night to enjoy.

Caleb rode his bike through the cold evening air. His costume crackled with each turn of the pedals, and he began to sweat. His mother had wrapped aluminum foil around an old sweater and pair of jeans, making him look more like the Tin Man than he did an astronaut. He wore a football helmet that he had painted silver with some paint his grandpa used for the roof of his outbuilding.

Caleb illuminated the road when he passed under

each street lamp. He slowed his bike at Marlee's driveway and felt his chest tighten when he saw the nurse on the porch. Was Marlee or someone sick?

The lady walked to the rail and waved. "Like my costume? I'm Clara Barton. You know, she started the Red Cross." Marlee was dressed in an all-white uniform, right down to the stockings and shoes. This was the first time Caleb had seen Marlee with her hair up in a bun. It was twisted tightly in the back, and a real nurse's cap was perched on top of her head. Her slender neck reached delicately into the stiff collar of her uniform. Caleb sat on his bike, mesmerized by the sight of Marlee. He couldn't believe how grown up she looked.

Marlee's mother stopped them on the porch steps for a photograph. "This'll be your last year, so let me take a picture. Stand over by the pun'kin. Y'all stand close and hold still. Say cheese!" She held the brownie camera at her waist, looking down into the viewfinder. There was a bright flash from the bulb in the silver bell, and Caleb saw spots for the next several minutes.

"And who are you, Caleb?" Mrs. Patterson asked.

"I'm Alan Shepard, the astronaut."

"Oh, yeah, I remember readin' somethin' about him. Well, you kids have fun. Don't be out late. It's a school night, you know."

They walked up the road toward the churchyard where Caleb had told Albert Whitfield to meet him.

"Why did you tell Albert he could go with us?" Marlee complained.

"He's been buggin' me all week about our Halloween plans. I got tired of tryin' to think up somethin', so I told him he could go."

Marlee crossed her arms and stomped her foot on

29

the wooden floorboards of the porch.

Caleb handed Marlee her canvas candy bag. "C'mon. I'm one of Albert's only friends. It won't be that bad. He's waiting at the church."

Albert and his younger sister, Alice, were sitting on the church steps when Caleb and Marlee arrived. Albert was dressed in ragged clothes and had a bandana tied on a stick, resting across his shoulder. Shoe polish served as a beard.

"Whoa!" Albert said when he saw Caleb. He held his hand to shield his eyes. "We ain't gonna lose you tonight! Who are you supposed to be, the Tin Man?"

When he looked at Marlee, his round face reddened. "You look nice, Marlee." Albert smiled; his dimples embedded into his chubby cheeks.

Marlee flashed a slight grin, then looked away, nervously adjusting her nurse's uniform.

Albert was also in the ninth grade, and his infatuation with Marlee was no secret, especially since last summer Alice, using red sidewalk chalk, had written "Albert Loves Marlee" on the walkway in front of the church.

"Sorry that squirt here had to tag along," Albert grumbled.

Alice was dressed as a fairy tale princess. She swatted at her brother with her candy bag.

"I think she's a beautiful princess. She's sure prettier than you!" Marlee said, twisting her back to Albert. Marlee took Alice by the hand, and the girls walked down Cane Creek Road, leaving the boys behind.

About an hour later, the four had combed all the streets on their side of the creek. They stood on the Cane Creek bridge surveying their loot.

"Wow, that'll last me for weeks!" Albert buried his head into the bulging grocery bag.

"Mine's so heavy I can hardly carry it. Hey, I got an apple!" Alice held it up and inspected it in the pale light of the street lamp.

Marlee slowly walked toward the end of the bridge. The thin dirt road that led to the hollow twisted into the tall pines and was swallowed by the dark nothingness beyond.

"Let's go down to the holler," Marlee said, still gazing into the darkness.

"You're crazy! Ain't no way I'm goin' down there, 'specially at night." Albert carried the stick over his shoulder, and the bandana shook, keeping time with his head. "No sirree. Not me!"

Caleb studied Marlee's face. Sometimes, he just couldn't figure her out. Had she suggested this so that she would look like the adventurer, knowing that no one would really go? At times, he would call her bluff, but not tonight. If she was remotely serious, he didn't want to take a chance of going to the hollow, especially on Halloween night.

Suddenly, the road lit up with bouncing headlights. An old truck labored to make it up the hill and onto the narrow bridge. Caleb recognized the grinding of the gears and rattling tailgate.

"That's Smoky! Let's get outta here!"

The four trick-or-treaters bolted off the bridge and ran into the field beside Cane Creek. They turned and saw the moonlight reflecting from the pale, ghost-like skin of Smoky Pruitt. A cigarette hung from his lip, and the glare from his haunting eyes cut through Caleb as if he had reached out his bony hand and swung a knife. The bawl of several hounds escaped from an old wooden crate in the back of the truck. Caleb shivered.

Smoky's truck turned on Cane Creek Road, away from town, toward the mountains.

"Wonder where he's goin'?" Albert asked.

"He looked scary. Let's go home, okay?" Alice whined.

"I bet he's going coon hunting." Caleb looked at the moon. It was much higher and smaller now, yet it still cast a fine shadow from the trees. "It's a good night for it."

Marlee tossed her head. "There's never a good night for hunting poor animals. C'mon, Alice, let's go."

Marlee reached for Alice's hand and turned to cross the bridge.

"I don't want to go down there." Alice began to cry. "That man scares me!"

"Well, he went off toward the mountain." Marlee patted Alice on the shoulder. "It'll be okay. He's gone."

"No! I don't want to!" Alice crossed her arms and clenched her fist.

"Uh oh, here comes a fit." Albert put both hands over his ears. "Listen, you scaredy cat li'l squirt, if you don't get—"

"Quit being an ol' meanie," Marlee interrupted. She reached again for Alice's hand. "We won't go down to the holler. Let's go to my house by the Cane Creek path. Then my daddy can drive y'all home.

She pointed down the hill to the trail that ran along the dark ribbon of water.

"What? Walk home in the woods, at night?" Albert backed up toward the road as he spoke.

The two girls started down the hill toward the trail,

their clasped hands swinging between them. Marlee looked over her shoulder at the boys who were still standing next to the bridge. "Now look who's the scaredy cat!" The girls' laughter faded as they rounded the first bend by the creek.

"C'mon," Caleb urged. "We can't let them go alone. There'll be plenty of light with the moon, and it's a shortcut to Marlee's house."

The boys followed behind, occasionally catching a glimpse of Marlee's white uniform and Alice's tiara before they dropped into the darkness of the next bend. The trees on both sides of the path loomed over their heads like folded skeleton hands. Caleb looked at the water and noticed the bright circle of the moon following them, dancing along the rocks in Cane Creek. Albert hadn't said a word, but his breath was coming quickly.

Just then, the girls ran around the curve to meet the boys.

"We heard something in the creek up ahead, splashing around!" Marlee whispered. Alice clung to Marlee's waist, burying her face in the white uniform.

"Yeah, yeah, now you're tryin' to scare us. Well, it ain't workin'!" Albert leaned forward, his jaw jutting out and his lips tightening.

"No, really, we heard something run along the creek bank and then splash in the water." Marlee's eyes were wide as she pointed her white sleeve toward the creek.

Caleb had seen Marlee when she was trying to pull a prank, and she could never do it without laughing. He knew that this time, she was serious.

"Okay, okay! Maybe it was a deer or something. C'mon, we'll all walk together." Caleb walked ahead of them up the trail.

The group moved silently, listening to every dry leaf rustling in the night breeze and jumping each time a ground squirrel scampered across the forest floor. Eventually, the trail turned away from the creek and emptied into Thompson's meadow that bordered the Patterson's property.

"Wow, I'm glad we're outta there!" Albert looked over his shoulder at the dark trail behind them.

Before long, they were chatting about their Halloween loot and laughing at each other's costumes.

Without warning, the brush border of the meadow exploded with a stir of commotion. The specters crashed through the hedgerow, yelling and waving their arms like wild creatures.

Alice dropped to the ground and screamed. She held her arms tightly over her head and buried her face into the damp meadow grass.

"What in the…Bobby Henderson! I oughta smack you!" Marlee yelled. Bobby and his friend Stephen bent over with laughter. Caleb rushed to Marlee's side while Albert backed up toward the trail.

"Oh, we got y'all good!" Bobby laughed, pointing his finger at the group.

"That wasn't funny!" Marlee stuck her hands on her hips, but she giggled as she walked over to Bobby. "You about scared me half to death splashing in the creek back there."

"You crazy? We didn't go in any creek. You must've heard a ghost." Bobby waved his hands over his head and rolled his eyes. Marlee laughed.

Bobby was always pulling some stunt and laughing at others' expense. Marlee had told Caleb on several occasions that Bobby was nothing but a spoiled brat, yet he noticed how she always giggled and blushed when Bobby was around. It was obvious to Caleb that Bobby was jealous of Caleb and Marlee's friendship. At church and school, Bobby would flirt with Marlee and make fun of Caleb in front of her. What bothered Caleb the most was how Marlee reacted to Bobby. She would pretend to be irritated at Bobby's antics, but Caleb knew Marlee so well. She couldn't hide that she enjoyed the attention.

Caleb turned and helped Alice to her feet. He clenched his teeth but didn't say a word. Bobby walked over to Alice. "Hey, pipsqueak, whatcha got in the bag?" He reached and snatched Alice's trick-or-treat sack from her hand.

"Hey, gimme that back!"

Bobby dropped the bag on the grass, but not before taking the large red apple from inside. "Look what I found. The pipsqueak got a baseball!" He threw the apple to Stephen.

"That's my only apple! Give it back!" Alice whined, folding her arms and poking out her lip.

Bobby and Stephen tossed the apple back and forth in a game of keep away.

"Bobby! Stop that." Marlee chuckled as she stepped beside the boy.

"Hey, Miss Nursey." Bobby reached and took Marlee's hand. "Why don't we go for a walk and play doctor?"

Just then, Stephen threw the apple, and it whizzed by Bobby and Marlee, bouncing past the trail and into the darkness. They heard a splash in the creek.

Alice began to cry.

Caleb felt his face tighten. He couldn't stand it any longer. "Now, see what you've done!" Caleb picked up his candy bag and football helmet and started walking toward the top of the meadow. He motioned to Albert, who was still standing at the wood's edge. "Let's get outta here."

Marlee started to follow, but Bobby grabbed her arm and pulled her back to his side.

"Hey, Austin, or should I say Tin Foil Man? Aren't you forgetting your girlfriend?"

In the moonlight, Caleb could see the blush on Marlee's face.

Then, the rage boiled up inside him. He turned and charged at Bobby, sending them both crashing into the meadow grass. All that could be seen was a flurry of aluminum foil and blond hair as the two boys rolled through the field like a wheel on a hay baler.

Marlee screamed for them to quit fighting while Albert and Stephen egged the two on. But their voices were drowned out by the sounds of punching and scuffling. Soon, the sound of fists and foil stopped.

Bobby jumped to his feet.

"My new jeans better not be torn, or you're gonna pay for 'em, you stupid hick!" Bobby stormed up the meadow path with Stephen following behind, patting him on the back.

Caleb sat in the meadow and brushed the remaining bits of aluminum foil from his grass-stained sweater. He could feel his eye swelling where Bobby had hit him, but he didn't say anything. Albert was picking up Caleb's candy bag and looking around for anything else that might have spilled.

"Caleb, you know I don't like fighting." Marlee flipped her head around. "C'mon, Alice, let's head on to my house."

There was no answer. Alice stood near the creek bank, holding something in her hand.

"How did you get your apple?" Albert asked. "I thought I heard it splash in the water."

Alice pointed across the creek to the field on the other side. "That girl gave it to me."

As the four children stood in the meadow, they could see the ghostly silhouette of a small girl traipsing across the moonlit field as she disappeared into the dark woods that led to the hollow.

Chapter 4

Caleb lay in bed with a bread bag containing ice cubes pressed against his swollen eye. Earlier that evening, he rode his bike home from Marlee's house with one eye closed. As soon as his mother saw his torn costume and battered cheek, she demanded an explanation. Caleb described his fight with Bobby Henderson, and all his father had to say was, "I hope you got in a few good licks!" Caleb said he did. His dad was satisfied. His mother gently inspected his swelling face, and when she was sure that no damage was done to his eye, she sent him straight to bed with a homemade cold compress.

Caleb balanced the ice bag on his face and sucked on a grape lollipop from his candy bag. This was not how he had hoped his final night of tick-or-treating would go. As he lay on his bed staring at the ceiling with one good eye, he recalled last Halloween. After trick-or-treating, he and Marlee sat on her porch swing and took inventory of their loot, trading candy and laughing at each other's costumes. Caleb had dressed as Superman and Marlee had dressed as the witch from the "Wizard of Oz," the good witch, of course.

But tonight was different. After crossing the meadow, Albert and Alice followed Caleb and Marlee to Marlee's house. Alice protested when Albert refused Marlee's offer to have her father drive them home. Caleb and Marlee stood on her porch and watched the two shuffle down Cane Creek Road toward their house, arguing the whole way. When they were out of sight, Marlee turned to Caleb.

"I better be going on in."

"But don't you want to look at our candy and trade?" Caleb opened his candy bag, inspecting the contents.

"I don't think so. I need to help my mama make cards for all the families of church members who died this year. Next Sunday is All Saints Day at church, remember?"

"Yeah, but…"

"Goodnight. See ya tomorrow at school." Marlee went inside and left Caleb standing alone on the porch, his candy sack drooping against his leg.

In bed, Caleb turned on his side and peered into his bag, but he wasn't hungry for anything else. He felt his stomach tighten, and his eye hurt. Caleb lifted the ice bag and touched the swelling. It seemed to be a little better. What would he tell kids at school when they saw his black eye? He did not doubt that Bobby Henderson would make up a big tale about their fight. He replaced the cold bag and peered out his window into the darkness. Why did Marlee like Bobby Henderson? All he ever does is make fun of people and try to be a big show-off. So, he comes from a rich family. Who cares? Marlee has always been interested in helping unfortunate people. She collected food for the needy and tried to make friends with the disadvantaged kids at school. She even wanted to help Annabelle Pruitt, so why does she like Bobby Henderson? He is the opposite of everything Marlee likes. These thoughts rolled through Caleb's head until he finally drifted off to sleep with a melting ice bag on his face.

****

"Wait up, Caleb!" Marlee yelled. School had let out, and Caleb was walking toward his home, burdened by several textbooks bound tightly with a strap. He felt like the teachers gave more homework between Halloween and Thanksgiving than at any other time of the school year. Several days had passed since Halloween, and Caleb had made it a point not to wait on Marlee after school was over.

Marlee trotted beside Caleb. He didn't look at her. "Why are ya in such a hurry? You didn't wait on me for the last two days? What's going on?"

Caleb shrugged. "Lots of homework, I guess."

"I wanted to ask you something about Halloween night. By the way, your eye looks almost normal."

"I'm fine," Caleb said sharply. He turned and looked behind them. "Where's your best buddy, Bobby?"

Marlee grabbed Caleb's arm and twisted him toward her. "What do you mean? Bobby's just a spoiled brat."

Caleb felt a smile build inside him, but his face never betrayed his thoughts.

"I hated how he treated Alice Halloween night, but I didn't think you needed to start a fight about it," Marlee continued.

Caleb wanted to tell Marlee that the fight was about *her*, not Alice. But he remained silent. He wished he could forget the entire incident.

"But I guess Bobby deserved it," Marlee added. "You know, I've been thinking. Who do you think handed Alice her apple? Do you think it was Annabelle? It was dark, and I didn't get a good look."

Caleb shook his head. "Maybe, but it could have

40

been anyone. It was Halloween night. Lots of kids out."

"Yeah, but I like to think it was Annabelle." Before Caleb could comment, Marlee took a few steps ahead of him. "Let's get a Dr. Pepper at Harper's…race ya!" Marlee took off running; her blonde hair flowing.

Caleb hesitated, shook his head, and smiled, and then, in a flash, caught up with Marlee. The two friends ran down Cane Creek Road, laughing all the way.

Chapter 5

The old floorboards of Caleb's grandparents' frame house creaked when he stepped onto the back porch. The house sat on what used to be a farm owned by Jeremiah Austin, Caleb's grandpa, until several years ago when he had deeded the entire parcel over to Caleb's father, who would one day give it to Caleb.

Caleb glanced around at the clutter of boots, sacks of potatoes, and a tangle of fishing rods stuck into an old bucket before peering through the backdoor glass into the kitchen. He wiped his feet on the rubber welcome mat and opened the door.

Caleb paused and breathed in deeply. Their kitchen always smelled good. He often wondered if his grandma slept there because he could usually find her wrapped in a flowery apron, baking, cooking, or canning some fruit or vegetable. In the summer, she may be in the garden tending to her "kitchen crops," as she called them, but in the winter, she darted around the large room, shuffling pans and sifting flour, creating wonderful aromas of baked bread and pastries. But today was Sunday. She spent most of her Sunday afternoons sitting in the parlor on a plastic-covered sofa, knitting a blanket she had stretched across the lap of her Sunday dress.

"The Lord's Day is for doing things that relax you. And for praying," Caleb had heard her say many times.

He grinned. Grandpa was definitely doing that. He

was stretched out in his vinyl recliner, asleep. His glasses were perched crooked across his face, his tie loosened and shifted to the side, and the Bible open across his belly, resting too.

"Why, Caleb. C'mon in, child," Grandma said, her bright eyes dancing. "How's that eye of yours? Your mama told me about that little scuffle you had Halloween night." She cocked her head so she could see out of her bifocals better.

"It's fine, Grandma." Caleb sat in front of his grandpa on the braided cord rug.

A small fire glowed in the fireplace, giving the room an inviting feel. The mantle held various family photographs, and the walls displayed an old painting of Jesus descending from heaven.

Caleb's grandpa snorted softly and straightened himself in the chair. He opened his eyes and adjusted his glasses. "Well, hello there, young man. I was just reading through the scriptures a little. How you comin' along?"

"You must've been getting the scriptures from the Lord himself! "Grandma teased, winking at Caleb.

"How's that eye? I hear you took quite a shiner a few days ago."

"It's all better. The swelling was gone the next day."

"Good, good. I've been waitin' for you to come help me get the woodpile ready."

"That's what I came to ask you. I could help you some today if you want."

"Now, you two had better not be going back there and splitting wood. Not on a Sunday, anyways." Grandma peered over her glasses at Grandpa.

"Oh, don't go get in a dither. I just want the boy to help me get the woodshed in shape for winter. That's not really work. Then, I can keep you warm as toast." Grandpa rubbed his hands together and nodded toward the fireplace.

"His ol' bones get cold too. That's really why he wants to get it ready." Grandma smiled and continued her sewing. "And be sure to stack some on the back porch. I don't want to go all that way out to the shed when the fire needs tending to."

Grandpa laughed. "We always do, just for you, old woman."

"Dear Gussie! Who's it that always complains 'bout his shoulders when he has to go out to the shed for wood?"

Grinning, Caleb leaned back to watch the good-natured banter between his grandparents. In his mind, he could hear his grandma say, "After sixty years together, you either learn to love 'em or kill 'em! And I've kept him around this long, so I may as well love him!"

Caleb followed his grandpa out the back door to the woodshed, a lean-to shelter connected to an outbuilding. They stood to survey the various sizes and types of wood. Most people might see the woodpile as a disheveled collection of dead limbs, an arbor bone yard. But Caleb knew better. For the last three years, he had helped his grandpa sort, stack, and select the wood. This was far from menial labor. Grandpa approached the skill of fire building as an almost spiritual event, and he was the master of the fire, Caleb's mentor.

Grandpa sorted through a pile of old pine knots. "Remember what these are?"

"Those are for startin' fires, the fat lighter, I think you called them."

"That's right. If you trim off a little of this, the ol'

sap inside will burn like a candle." Grandpa cut a slice with his pocketknife, exposing the pungent yellowish wood beneath the scaly pine bark. "How about stackin' this red oak I cut yesterd'y? Put it over there on the far end."

"Yessir," Caleb said. He had learned that the woodpile was organized not only by size and type of wood but also by age and use.

"You aren't going to use this wood till next year, right?" Caleb asked.

"That's 'bout right. That oak'll be some good burnin' next year, but I'll mix a li'l in now and then. It makes a fire burn longer if'n you put some grccn in with it."

Caleb sat down an armload. "You know everythin' about buildin' a fire, don't you, Grandpa?"

"I'll tell you, Caleb, once upon a time, we had to heat this whole house with wood. That's why you see all the fireplaces. We didn't have oil heat like we do today. Now we build a fire just to knock the chill outta the air." Grandpa sat on a stump and straightened his work gloves. "Your grandma and I had this house built back in 1906. Then we started raisin' our family. Your daddy was the last to be born here. He was kinda a latecomer."

Although he had seen several faded pictures of the tall, thin, broad-shouldered man, Caleb couldn't imagine his grandpa as a young man. All grandpas were old and had always been old. Whenever his grandpa talked about his childhood in the late 1880s, it seemed more like an adventure tale than the life of a real person.

"Yep, my boy, I've built a lot of fires in this ol' house," Grandpa said, looking at the back porch, reminiscing. He leaned over and picked up a stick of firewood. "You know, Caleb, wood warms you in three ways. It warms your body when you cut it, it warms your body when you burn it, and it warms your soul when you look at the fire."

Caleb grinned, thinking about his grandpa's words. He wrinkled his forehead and took a seat on a split log. "Were you real poor in the old days?"

"Well, I guess that depends. When I was younger, we didn't have all the things we do today, but then, not too many people did."

"You had an outhouse, didn't you?"

"Yes, we did. I tell you, boy, you can't appreciate indoor plumbin' until you've gone to the outhouse on a cold, windy winter night!" He slapped his leg and let out a bellowing laugh. "We used to keep hogs over there behind that buildin', and I'd string them up from that ol' hickory tree to kill 'em. Chickens for eggs, and a cow named Betsy. Yep, we didn't need a grocery store back then, 'cept for a few things we couldn't make ourselves."

"Why don't you still have them all?" Caleb asked.

"Well, your daddy took care of the farm until he went off to the war. I took a factory job and just didn't have the time or energy to keep it all up."

"I remember the chickens. You just got rid of them a couple of years ago." Caleb pointed to the old coop where the rusty chicken wire strained across the leaning frame.

"Yep, and I still have some of my bees up in the orchard near the apple trees. As a matter of fact, I need to go check on 'em before the hard cold gets here. I haven't been up there in a spell. Might even find us an apple or two." Grandpa put one hand on his knee, and grunting, he pushed himself up from his seat.

****

The trained branches of the apple trees stood like gnarled beasts guarding the woods beyond. At the edge of the tree line, several white hives sat next to each other like miniature skyscrapers, each four supers tall. Grandpa had picked up an old smoker can from the outbuilding and handed it to Caleb.

"Go up there under the trees and stuff some pine needles in here. That's about the best thing for smokin' these varmints, even though I don't think they're movin' much now that it's gotten a little chilly."

Caleb made a wide sweep at the top of the orchard to avoid the hives. He filled the can with pine needles and followed the same path back to where his grandpa stood under the apple trees.

"Good man! Now let's get it lit and see what these li'l boogers are up to." Grandpa dug deep into his pocket for his shiny silver-colored lighter. He gave it a flick and touched the flame to the clump of pine needles sticking from the top of the smoker. With the handle compressed, smoke streamed from the top of the old gray can and swirled around in the air before fading among the craggy limbs of the apple tree. Caleb waved his hand in front of his face. "Why do they like *that* smell?"

"Oh, they don't like it at all." Grandpa ambled around the hives and puffed streams of smoke into the entrances. "It scares them. It makes them think there's a forest fire or somethin'. Then they gorge their little bellies with honey and get quiet. Kinda like me after Sunday dinner!" Grandpa laughed and stepped back, letting the smoke flow into the hive.

"You're not afraid they'll sting you?" Caleb took a few steps back as his grandpa lifted the top off the first super.

"Aw, I'm just gonna take a peek. If it was warmer and I was goin' to do some serious hivin', I'd tie my sleeves and pants legs and wear my veil on my head. That'd protect me from the bees and the smoke. Come look here." Grandpa carefully slid one of the frames out of the white box for Caleb to see the honey-filled wax cones. "Most of it has already been robbed, but there's a li'l left." The bees huddled over the frame as Grandpa broke off a piece of wax. "Here, try this. Won't find anythin' any better in Harper's candy case, that's for sure!"

Caleb slipped beside his grandpa and took the chunk of wax from his hands. It dripped with light-colored sourwood honey. He slid it in his mouth and chewed it like bubble gum. The thick honey oozed from the firm wax and filled his mouth with a delicious sweetness.

"What's robbed them already?" Caleb asked, licking his fingers.

Grandpa popped the top off the next hive. "I don't do much with them anymore. I let the colored man across the woods, Mr. Williams, tend to them mostly. He takes care of 'em and brings me a few jars of honey."

Caleb walked back to the orchard, chewing on the sweet wax while his grandfather secured the last hive, the smoke still making gray whips from the top of the can he was carrying.

"Once, back when your daddy was about your age, we had this whole hillside full of hives. Of course, we had a lot more trees then, too. The bees help by pollinatin' the apple trees. Without them, we wouldn't have any fruit." Grandpa reached up and balanced himself on an apple limb. "Got my whole stock of bees from J.B. Pruitt. He'd find a hive down in the holler, rob it, and sell the bees."

"Pruitt? Like Smoky Pruitt?" Caleb asked.

"Yep. That's J.B.'s son. Well, actually, Charles is Smoky's real name." The can had almost stopped smoking except for an occasional trace escaping from under the lid. Grandpa carefully placed the smoker on the ground and took a seat under one of the old apple trees. "You better make sure you don't knock over the smoker, or you'll get a nickname for life." Grandpa adjusted his back against the rough bark of the tree and chuckled.

"Charles? Smoky's name is really Charles?" Caleb sat on the ground beside his grandpa.

"You see, Charles was his name until one day years ago. J.B. sent word to me that he had a good-sized swarm of bees in a tree down by Cane Creek. I guess your daddy was about sixteen or so, and Charles was just a year or two behind him. Anyways, your daddy and I went down there to get the bees. J.B. had let Charles do the smokin'. When he finished, he set the can in some dry grass and plopped himself right down next to it, just like this." Caleb's grandpa began to shake his head and laugh. "While we were busy gettin' the bees out of a big sourwood tree, the grass caught fire along with the backside of Charles's overall britches. He took to hollerin' and ran straight into the woods with smoke pourin' out his rear end. The next sound we heard was a big splash where he had jumped into Cane Creek. Straightaway, I told J.B. that he had done gone and let his best smoker fall in the creek. I'll tell you from that day on, he's been called Smoky by ever'body, friend, and foe!"

"I always thought he got the name 'cause he smoked…animals and stuff."

"Maybe that's why he took up that trade of smokin' hams. You never know. Boy, I can still see him tearin' off toward the creek, hobblin' at the way with that limp of his. He sure looked a sight!"

"He walked with a limp way back then?" Caleb asked.

Grandpa reached and plucked a tall piece of grass and put it in his mouth. "Oh yeah. I think he was born with one leg a li'l shorter than the other. That's what kept him outta the army. When all the other boys, like your daddy and uncles, went off to the war, he had to stay behind. Kinda took some of the air outta him."

"Seems like he'd be happy." Caleb pulled a blade of grass and began to chew on it like his grandpa.

"Caleb, durin' the world wars, and I've lived through both, a man was proud to serve his country. If he couldn't, well, he felt kinda ashamed, kinda like he'd let folks down."

Caleb lay back in the grass with his hands behind his head, chewing on a stalk of grass, and looked through the tangled limbs of the apple trees. "Wonder if I'll ever have to fight in a war?"

Grandpa let out a long, slow breath and shook his head slowly. "Son, I sure pray you don't. I've been lucky to have all my boys come home. Not ever'body could say that."

Grandpa fumbled in his shirt pocket and pulled out a pack of Camel non-filtered cigarettes. He thumped one out of the pack and put it in the corner of his mouth. Leaning, he dug into his pants for the shiny lighter, all the while eyeing Caleb. "Now don't you go tellin' your grandma. I only smoke them when I've been burnin' somethin'." He nodded toward the smoker as he flicked the lighter wheel. "That way, she won't smell it and conk me with a fryin' pan."

Caleb chuckled as he sat up on one elbow. He watched the end of the cigarette glow brightly as his grandpa sucked in the smoke. Caleb waited for what seemed like forever until his grandpa blew the long, gray stream out of his mouth and nose. The lines on the old man's face seemed deeper than usual, like a road map. Through squinted eyes, his expression grew strangely somber. He looked across the orchard to the wood beyond.

"You know, in lots of ways, I can understand ol' J.B. Pruitt. His oldest boy was killed overseas during the war."

"Smoky's brother was killed?"

"J.B. took to drankin' and quit doin' just about anythin' after that." There was a long pause before he spoke again. "I remember when my first boy died." Grandpa snuffed out his cigarette in the dry dirt.

"That was Samuel, right?"

He looked up as if startled to hear his dead son's name spoken. "Yeah. It was that danged Spanish flu. It took a lot of folks before their time. Kinda like war, I guess. Anyhow, Smoky's brother became a little bit of a hero around here. Lookin' back on it, I think that part hurt Smoky the most."

"What part?" Caleb sat up cross-legged and plucked another piece of grass.

"Well, I don't think Smoky quite ever measured up to his brother. Not in J.B.'s eyes, anyways. Smoky had to work to put food on their table. Not too long after, his mama ran off, and then his daddy just drank himself into the grave."

"What did Smoky do with no folks around?"

"He was a young man by that time. He started paintin' houses and was pretty good at it, so folks say. He married a girl from over in Arden and was doin' well, but then his wife took sick after bein' in the family way and died. You know, bad things always seem to follow some folks around. All he does now is smoke those hams and drink liquor. At least that's what I'm told, anyways."

"He's got Annabelle and maybe another daughter, according to Marlee," Caleb added.

"Seems like that should be enough to keep a man goin'. Speakin' of goin', your grandma's gonna have the sheriff out lookin' for us. C'mon, let's get some wood for her fire."

The two walked down the slope toward the woodshed, each quiet in thought.

****

Grandpa hung the smoker in the outbuilding while Caleb selected the proper-sized sticks for his grandma's fireplace. He unrolled a piece of old canvas in front of the woodshed. The musty fabric was worn thin from years of toting wood to the house. The smell reminded him of the times his daddy and grandpa had taken him camping in an old army tent on the upper end of Pinner's Creek.

After laying the wood down, he folded the canvas and put his hands through the slits cut in the top for carrying. The bundle slapped against his leg as he walked to the house. Caleb was ready to tend to the sacred art of fire building.

Chapter 6

The smell of bacon and the rattle of a spoon stirring grits were the usual wake-up call on weekends at the Austin house. But this was not Saturday. This was Thanksgiving Day, and there were turkeys to smoke. Caleb gulped down his breakfast, pulled on his wool coat, and darted through the door toward his grandparents' house.

Caleb breathed in the cold mountain air as he ran past his neighbors' houses. In their small community, everyone shared their lives with neighbors. Caleb knew every family member, as well as their dogs and cats on his street.

Mrs. Miller, wrapped in a pink quilted housecoat, was sweeping her front porch. She waved at Caleb and then glanced up the road. Her son and his family were driving from Knoxville for Thanksgiving and should be pulling up any time. Caleb ran past the Johnsons' house and let his knit glove streak along the frost-covered window of a car parked on the street. The Johnsons' family had arrived the night before. Now he could see the first lights coming on inside the house. Smoke from their chimney made a straight trail before disappearing into the cold, blue sky.

Caleb cut across his grandparents' meadow through a path of trampled grass. He loved cold mornings in Fletcher. The Queen Anne's lace bowed her dried flowers, and small spider webs decorated with drops of melting frost reflected the sunlight like tiny crystals. He inhaled the air and then exhaled slowly, savoring the aroma of this time of year. Every breath of the cold, clean air carried a new autumn smell. The earthy odor of dried oak leaves raked into mulch beds gave way to the sweet fragrance of freshly bailed hay spotting the fields along the road. He could have continued his run through the field and eventually along Cane Creek and Thompson's Meadow, enjoying all that the morning had to offer, but that journey would have to wait for another day.

Grandpa was cleaning the grill of his smoker when Caleb bounded through an opening in the privet hedgerow. Smoke streamed out of the chimney, and Caleb could see his grandma through the window, her hands deep in a bowl of dressing, preparing for the family meal later that day.

"Hello there, young man!" Grandpa greeted. "Bring me that bag of charcoal beside the steps."

Caleb hoisted the twenty-pound bag onto his shoulder and carried it to where his grandpa cleaned the smoker. A fifty-five-gallon drum, resting on a wall of concrete blocks, made up the body of the smoker. Years ago, Grandpa had welded hinges, a handle, and a smokestack onto the drum. For as long as Caleb could remember, his grandpa had smoked turkeys for Thanksgiving as well as the Christmas social at church.

Now Caleb was to learn the smoking process.

"Where're the turkeys?" Caleb asked as he set the charcoal beside the smoker.

"Your grandma has them inside. We started thawing them Tuesday night. I got three nice ones this year, both on the edge of McHenry's cornfield."

"Wish I could've gone with you." Caleb picked up a small coffee can of water. He remembered the use of water in the smoking process from last year.

"I wish you could've gone too, but it was a school day, and I was out before the sun came up. But you'll get your chance soon enough," Grandpa replied.

"Are you ready for the hickory chips?"

"No, that'll be a while yet. Go on over to the pile and pick me out five or six chips, but keep them soakin'. We don't want them to dry out."

Caleb chose five pieces of hickory wood "about as long as a man's finger and as round as his thumb," as his grandpa had always instructed him, and placed them in the water.

"The wood won't be put on the coals until they're white hot. I'll do that a li'l later."

"Next week, I'm goin' with Daddy out to Smoky's place to pick up the hams for the church social. Do you think ol' Smoky is out doin' this right now with his hams?" Caleb gave his grandpa the old coffee can with the wet hickory chips inside.

"No, he killed those hogs last year. It takes several months to cure them before he puts them in the smokehouse."

"I never knew why they called it curing. Are the pigs sick or something?" Caleb joked.

Grandpa chuckled at the idea. "No, no, that just means they're preserved. That way, they won't go bad. When it's cold enough, he'll kill the hog and then take the legs and rub salt and sugar into them. That's what cures them."

"I thought the smoke did that, like with your turkeys."

"The smoke gets credit for somethin' it doesn't do. It only adds flavor to the meat. The heat from the coals cooks the bird, but hams are cured with salt and sugar."

Grandpa poured lighter fluid on the charcoal and then struck a wooden match. They stood around the blaze, warming their hands from the cold morning air. "The hams y'all are goin' to get next Saturday were smoked last spring and kept in a root cellar or somewhere cool."

"So, he only smokes the legs? What does he do with the rest of the pig?"

"Believe me; they use everythin' but the squeal!" The old man laughed as they huddled close to the charcoal fire to catch its warmth.

The coals piled to one side were now beginning to turn white. They could feel the heat increasing as more and more briquettes began to ignite. Grandpa reached beside the smoker and handed Caleb a metal pan. "Go over to the faucet and fill this with water. We have to put it in before we put the grill top on."

Caleb returned and carefully placed the pan into the smoker beside the hot coals. His eyes watering now, he stepped back, waving his hands.

"Good job. That's an important part of smokin'. I'll place the birds over the pan so they'll cook cooler and slower."

Caleb wiped his eyes with his glove. "Smoke sure smells good from a ways off, but up close, it can burn your eyes."

"Yep, smoke and fire can be used for good and bad things." Grandpa closed the lid. "You know, it's kinda strange. Like I said, the smoke gets all the credit. I mean, it's the heat, or salt if you're doin' hams, that does the curin'. The smoke is what folks see and taste, so it gets the credit."

Caleb's grandpa removed his glasses and wiped his stinging eyes with an old, tattered handkerchief. He then put one end of his glasses in his mouth and began to puff on the plastic frame like a pipe. He wrinkled his brow, staring at the sky.

"Yessir, Caleb. Smoke is kinda like all this stuff in our lives." He waved his arm around him, pointing his glasses at his woodshed and house. "It's all nice. It adds some flavor, but too much of it can smother you, put out the fire, so to speak." He pointed his glasses at Caleb as if teaching a lesson. "It's the fire that counts. After all, it makes the smoke, right?"

Caleb didn't answer. He wasn't exactly sure what his grandpa meant, but he knew it meant something.

"Let's go check on those turkeys." Grandpa rested his arm around Caleb's shoulders as they walked toward the back porch. "Yep, my boy, you better be careful. There's a lot of smoke in this world." The screen door banged behind them.

Chapter 7

It was the first Saturday in December, the day of the Christmas social at Fletcher First Baptist Church. Each year at Christmastime, some of the women's Sunday school class members prepared a dinner for the congregation and meals to take to less fortunate families. Caleb and Marlee's families were among the members who helped cook, package, and distribute these meals.

Mr. Patterson's old Chevy truck bounced down the dirt road, dodging tire ruts and potholes on its way to the hollow to pick up the hams from Smoky Pruitt. Caleb and Marlee sat in the truck bed, shoulder to shoulder, wrapped in their winter coats and caps with their knees pulled up under their chins. The cold wind stung their reddened cheeks. They could hear the muffled voices of their dads in the cab and occasionally caught glimpses of gray cigarette ashes being flicked out the window.

"Reckon we'll see her or maybe even get to talk to her?"

"Who?" Caleb asked, tossing a piece of pine bark left over from the last mulch haul into the air.

"Annabelle."

"Why'd we wanna do that? I don't even wanna see Smoky."

"You're not curious about her?"

"Nope. Just glad I'm not crazy like her."

"Who said she was crazy?" Marlee replied with

irritation in her voice.

"Henry, for one."

"Oh, you can't listen to that big ol' spitbelly!"

The truck hit a couple of ruts in the road, and the two grabbed each other to keep their balance. Caleb and Marlee's dads glanced over their shoulders and laughed. Mr. Patterson let out a faint cry, "Giddy-up!"

"Henry's not all that bad," Caleb said. "We all went shooting Thanksgiving afternoon. He taught me how to shoot a muzzleloader. It was so swell!" Caleb threw his hands up, holding an imaginary rifle, and aimed at the top of a pine tree.

"I know Henry's not *all* bad, but he'll tell you a tall tale and never set you straight. Mama calls that lyin'."

Caleb aimed at another pine tree with his make-believe muzzleloader. "You should've been there to see us."

Caleb hadn't expected Marlee to come with her dad and brother because he knew she hadn't been invited. Thanksgiving target practice was a tradition with the Austin men and their friends. That day, after the dinner had been cleared away and the ladies busied themselves with whatever the ladies do, the men sat on the porch polishing and admiring their guns. Caleb didn't own a gun, but he got to shoot just about every gun there.

As they sat in the truck bed, Caleb remembered the smell of gun oil that Thanksgiving afternoon. It was thick in the cool November air, and it was soon to be replaced by the pungent odor of burnt gunpowder.

Thanksgiving afternoon, Caleb's dad had parked his grandpa's pick-up truck on an old logging road next to Mr. Patterson and Henry. The men gathered in a clearing where they spent the afternoon tossing old bottles and lining up cans. With the deafening sounds of gunfire and the thick smoke caught in the limbs of the oak trees, Caleb felt an ancient pluck on the cord of brotherhood.

Thanksgiving was Caleb's first time to shoot a .12-gauge shotgun. At home the night before, Caleb's father had instructed him in the proper handling of the gun. Thinking back to that day, Caleb remembered his father simply handing him the gun and tossing him a couple of shells.

"See what you can do with it, son," he said, winking. To the other men, it appeared that Caleb was an old hand at shooting the shotgun. Caleb loaded the gun and pressed it firmly against his shoulder. He saw his grandpa poised, ready to throw the bottle into the air.

With nervous fingers and a deep breath, Caleb shouted, "Go!" When he pulled the trigger, sound and smoke completely engulfed him as the barrel of the gun flew straight up with the kick. The bottle exploded into a thousand pieces. Yells and applause from his friends and family replaced the thunderous boom from the shotgun. Caleb replayed that scene over and over in his head. He could still feel the slaps on his back from the men showing their pride in him.

Now, Marlee sat beside him, staring over the truck's tailgate as Caleb aimed his imaginary gun at trees and telephone poles.

"Why do you think she never comes to school, and why didn't she say anything that day when we saw her at Turtle Rock? And Halloween night, do you think she gave the apple back to Alice?" Marlee broke the silence and brought Caleb back from his imaginary target practice.

Half-listening, Caleb shrugged and took one more

shot at a single cloud in the blue sky.

"You know, Caleb, I know I'd be sad if my mama had died when I was a little kid like her. I think it did do something to her."

"Yeah, especially if what Henry said was true, you know, about the smokehouse and all."

"Land sakes, Caleb, like I told you, Henry is full of something, and it ain't brains!"

The truck slowed and made a right turn across Cane Creek Bridge as they entered the hollow. The dirt road followed the slope of the creek. The area didn't look nearly as ominous as it had on Halloween night. The scenery was quite nice. Caleb liked the creek here because the water flowed rapidly over large rocks and terraces and harbored hungry fish. This was one of the best trout stretches in the county. He and his dad had been fishing here a time or two, and they planned to come back one day soon. He hoped.

Small clearings appeared on the side of the road, planted with winter greens of turnips and collards, bordered by unpainted houses wanting repair. Several houses had children sitting on the porch or pushing each other in a tire swing strung from ancient oak trees.

In the front yard of one of the houses, Caleb watched two boys throwing what appeared to be a ball of burlap through a metal barrel ring nailed to the side of an outbuilding.

Caleb and Marlee rode quietly in the truck bed, studying the houses and watching the grown-ups who would stop their chores and stare at the passing truck. A few children would run along the side of the road and wave at Caleb and Marlee, who would shyly return the gesture. Caleb noticed the small outhouses perched at the wood's edge and remembered his grandpa saying that he had grown up using one. None of the trees along the road were threaded with power lines like they were in his part of town. He wondered if they had ever watched television or had a radio. Did anyone have a telephone?

Mr. Patterson turned away from the creek onto a narrow drive and stopped in front of the Pruitt house. It was identical in structure to the other homes in the hollow. They were sometimes called "salt boxes" because of their square shape. The unpainted wooden siding cracked around rusty nail heads, and the roof had several missing shingles. A large front porch struggled under several ladder-back chairs and a pile of firewood that took up most of the space on the porch. Caleb immediately noticed the organization of the wood. It seemed to be stacked according to its use, and it must have been the only source of heat for the house.

Before they had even come to a stop, four skinny hound dogs charged from under the porch and surrounded the truck, bawling, announcing the arrival of visitors. Mr. Patterson blew on his horn two times. Marlee pushed on Caleb's shoulder and stood up in the back of the truck as one of the dogs, tail wagging playfully, placed its front paws on the tailgate and looked over into the bed at the children.

"Hey there, fella." Marlee giggled as another dog jumped straight into the air and then fell back to the ground, its ears standing out like little parachutes. Caleb sat quietly, leaning against the cab, keeping his eyes on the front door of Smoky's cabin.

"Kids, don't touch 'em," Mr. Patterson said as a warning, his head bent out the truck window. "I'm sure they haven't had any shots." He started to open the door but then slammed it quickly when two of the dogs loped over, bawling and turning in circles beside the truck door.

"Git!" the man cried, clomping down the porch steps, clapping his hands with a resounding crack. The dogs retreated immediately, their tails tucked and heads lowered.

It was Smoky Pruitt.

Marlee lowered herself back down in the truck beside Caleb, almost as if the order to "git" was aimed at her. Marlee snuggled close to Caleb and leaned against the cab where their fathers sat. Caleb sat straight and placed his hand on Marlee's arm. They peered over the side of the truck bed as Smoky limped to the driver's side.

Smoky Pruitt was a tall, skinny man. His thin, gaunt face with protruding cheekbones and sunken eyes reminded Caleb of the skeleton at the school Halloween festival.

"Got yer hams. Y'all pull 'round yonder ta th' cold house," Smoky ordered, pointing a long, skinny finger up the hill to a building not much taller than Caleb.

The truck pulled away and bounced over the deep furrows in the trail. Caleb and Marlee held tight to the side and watched wide-eyed as Smoky ambled up the trail behind them. His thin legs poked out of his too-short overalls into a pair of untied hunting boots.

The cold house was a dirt cellar dug out of a flat area on the hillside. The small building was about ten feet square with a steep frame roof. As Mr. Patterson pulled his truck along the side of the cellar, Smoky lifted a thick wooden door off the front and laid it on the ground before disappearing into the dark beyond.

The men slid out of the truck, and Caleb's dad pulled down the tailgate. "Y'all come on down and stand out of the way."

Caleb stepped toward the cellar door, careful not to get near Smoky, and peered inside. The entire structure was one big hole with dirt sides and floor. Dim light found its way through the cracks in the sideboards, allowing Caleb to see small burlap-covered silhouettes hanging from soot-covered beams. He was relieved to find only hams. No dogs were suspended in the cold house. That was another one of Henry's tall tales proven wrong.

Suddenly, Smoky was at the door and thrust a ham into Caleb's chest. "Here, boy." Caleb stumbled and fell on one knee. His face twisted in horror as he stared at the burlap bundle pressed tightly against his chest. Just then, his dad leaned over, took the bundle from Caleb, and placed it in the back of the truck.

His jaw tightened, and his right eyebrow raised. "Y'all stand over there for now. We'll load, and you can help unload at the church," he said. Caleb's dad placed his hand on Caleb's shoulder and cut his eyes sharply at Smoky.

"Yessir." Caleb brushed the dirt off his knees and lowered his head, not looking at Marlee. He felt the warmth of his blush and knew that he must look like a ripe tomato.

Marlee stepped away from the truck and peered up a trail at a row of three cabin-like smokehouses. Cracked mud sealed the spaces between the logs, and a wood-shingled roof girded the small stone chimneys.

"They sure do a lot of smoking up here. I wonder if Annabelle helps her daddy with it?" Marlee said. Caleb moved beside her and saw that only one chimney had smoke rising from a crooked pipe.

"Smoking's not done this time of the year. This is the time for the killing and curing," Caleb added, proud of his knowledge. "The smoking comes later."

"So why is smoke coming from that cabin up there?" Marlee pointed up the trail to the last small house. It was set further into the hillside, slightly obscured by an evergreen thicket.

"Maybe Annabelle is up there. Let's go see." Marlee glanced at the men who were occupied loading hams into the truck bed. She started up the winding path leading to the smokehouses.

Caleb grabbed Marlee's arm and shook his head. "I don't think that's a good…"

Just then, the door of the little smokehouse opened, and Annabelle stepped out on the log steps. Without a word, Marlee pulled away from Caleb and marched up the path.

"Where're you going?" Caleb asked in a loud whisper. He wondered why he bothered to ask the question.

Marlee walked on, purpose in her stride. Caleb followed behind, unsure.

"But we might need to help them with the hams or somethin'."

"I wanna talk to Annabelle." Marlee didn't look back.

"Are you sure she can even…uh…talk?"

Marlee's body stiffened as she glanced over her shoulder at Caleb. He knew the look—that determined expression of Marlee on a mission. This was more than mere curiosity. For some reason, Marlee was always drawn to the underdog, and now she was drawn to Annabelle.

Caleb had seen her become acquainted with many of the kids at school when others simply had made fun of them. Last year, there was a girl who had always worn the same dirty pink dress. Marlee had sat beside her for one week at lunch and talked about almost everything, although the girl rarely talked back. And Caleb remembered the Cherokee boy with no friends and the girl who had never bathed and smelled bad. Marlee had sat beside them at snack time and picked them for her kickball team when she was captain. But Caleb had to admit that he often wondered if Marlee truly wanted to be their friend or if she simply found them interesting, like the odd characters they saw every year when the traveling carnival came through Arden. Of course, there was Bobby Henderson who was far from being needy. But Caleb couldn't think about that right now. He needed to keep Marlee from getting into trouble.

"I don't think this is such a good idea. Our daddies are about—"

Marlee continued up the path toward the smokehouse, leaving Caleb in mid-sentence with his hand pointing toward the three men loading hams into the truck.

****

Annabelle sat on the log steps and poked at the dirt with a stick while Marlee walked up and stopped several feet in front of her. Behind Marlee, Caleb slowly ambled up the trail. He recognized the smell of the smoke coming from the small house where Annabelle was sitting. No one smokes with pine wood, so why's it coming from that smokehouse? he thought.

"Hi, Annabelle," Marlee said.

Caleb stopped and stood sheepishly a few feet behind Marlee, watching.

Annabelle stared at the bare ground. She shifted her feet, stirring up little puffs of dust with her boots. She continued to draw circles in the dirt with the stick.

Her hair was shoulder-length and matted. Pieces of straw hung loosely in the brown tangles. Her dress, dirty and torn in several places, was long and too big for her thin frame. The ragged hem touched the tops of her laceless leather shoes.

"My name is Marlee, and this is my friend Caleb." Marlee reached behind her and tugged at Caleb's arm.

"Uh…hi," Caleb said, reluctantly. He wasn't sure what to say next, so he stood silent. He glanced down the hill at the men loading hams on the truck. Maybe they would finish soon.

Annabelle wrapped her arms around her chest and began to rock back and forth, still staring at the dirt.

"Come on, Marlee. I think they're finished gettin' the hams." Caleb started to walk down the path, relieved that this mission was over.

"Well, bye, Annabelle. We have to go." Marlee was polite, but Caleb could hear the disappointment in her voice. She turned and walked with Caleb toward the truck.

"I seed ya," Annabelle said in a hushed voice, not looking up and rocking faster than before. Marlee and Caleb both turned and stared at the girl on the steps.

"I seed ya down at th' store," Annabelle repeated, still not making eye contact.

Marlee turned and walked quickly back to where Annabelle was sitting.

"Oh, you saw us at Harper's Store?" Marlee asked.

There was no response. Marlee glanced at Caleb, who was still lingering on the path.

"We love to go down there. When'd you see us?" Marlee placed her hand behind her back and motioned for Caleb to stand beside her. He hesitated. He had never been around somebody like Annabelle and wasn't sure how to act. But he moved beside Marlee, who was trying to keep the conversation alive.

"Ya had th' brown candy, what ya holt to," Annabelle said, glancing up slightly and then looking back at her feet, still rocking herself.

Marlee paused for a second and searched Caleb's face; her brow wrinkled. Then she brightened. "Oh, yeah, the Sugar Daddies. They're good. They'll last all day long. Remember, Caleb?"

Caleb stood silent, staring at Annabelle. He didn't hear Marlee until she poked him in the ribs with her finger and spoke through clenched teeth.

"Don't they last all day, Caleb?"

"Oh…yeah…all day."

"Do you like to go to Harper's store? I know I do. They've lots of neat stuff," Marlee said.

Caleb could tell she was trying to think of something else to say, but he couldn't think of anything to add.

"I stay in th' truck. Papa goes in." Annabelle looked up only to say the words and then glanced away.

"Do you like Sugar Daddies? Or maybe you like…chewing gum…or candy canes?" Marlee glared at Caleb, widening her eyes and jerking her head, signaling for some help with the dying conversation.

"Had 'em once. They's good," Annabelle answered.

"Peppermint's my favorite. Is it yours, too?"

Annabelle didn't answer. She stopped drawing and tossed her stick toward the brook that flowed by the smokehouse.

"We saw you by the creek one day, a while back," Marlee said. There was no response from the girl. "We also saw you Halloween night. You gave Alice her apple. That was a sweet thing to do."

Annabelle glanced up at Marlee and then looked back at her feet. "I don't go down ta th' creek at night. Never at nightime."

Marlee wrinkled her brow and looked at Caleb, puzzled.

"We sure thought it was you."

"I don't go to no creek at night! Annabelle raised her voice defiantly.

"Well, anyway, we're having a Christmas social tonight at the church. That's why we're getting all the hams. We always have a social on the first Saturday in December." Marlee paused for some reaction from Annabelle. There was none.

Caleb looked at Marlee and shrugged. Marlee had done all she could do.

Marlee moved a little closer to where Annabelle was sitting. Her steps were slow and deliberate. "How would you like to go to the Christmas social, Annabelle? Do you think you could? Would you like that?"

Caleb's mouth flew open, but he had nothing to say. He just glared at Marlee. He was ready to support her efforts at making conversation, but to take this girl to the church social? Since Marlee had become president of her Sunday School class, she had received three ribbons for bringing the most people to church. She had them taped to the mirror on her dresser at home. But this was just too much. So, what if Marlee got another ribbon or maybe a truckload of ribbons? Maybe she could get so many she couldn't even see herself in her mirror. But Annabelle at their church? There was no way she would fit in with her dress, her hair, and the way she talked.

Annabelle pulled her knees up to her chest and began to make a ball out of the hem of her dress. She sat, wringing the material as if it were soaking wet.

"We're going back to decorate now. We have a Christmas tree and lots of food. And presents. We even set up a big manger scene in front of the church. I bring the doll for the baby Jesus." Marlee tossed her blonde curls back and smiled.

Annabelle stopped twisting her hem and looked straight at Marlee's face for the first time. "Ain't no baby, yet!"

"Oh…well…no, but we're going to set it up today. I'll bring the doll and—"

"Ain't no baby yet!" Annabelle said, even louder than before, slinging the hem of her dress to the ground.

Marlee and Caleb cut glances at each other. What in the world was she talking about? Caleb thought.

At that moment, Caleb's dad yelled from beside the truck. "Caleb! Time to go."

"Okay, Daddy." Caleb grabbed Marlee's coat sleeve and tugged. "Come on, Marlee."

Caleb was relieved to be going toward the truck. It was obvious to him that Annabelle was getting upset, even though he had no idea why. He started trotting down the hill, pulling Marlee with him.

"You git on in th' house, girl!" Smoky stood behind the truck and shouted at the little girl in the same tone he had used on the dogs earlier.

Annabelle jumped up like she had been struck with a switch and ran down the trail to the big house. She stopped abruptly and turned to look at Marlee and Caleb.

"Ain't no baby yet!" Caleb and Marlee watched her run into the old shack.

"What do you think she meant by that?" Caleb asked.

"I guess she knows we haven't put the doll in the—" Marlee stopped and turned toward the small smokehouse cabin where Annabelle had been sitting. "Did you hear that?"

"No, I didn't hear nothin'," Caleb said, a slight tremble in his voice.

"I thought I heard a voice come out of that cabin," Marlee said, squatting with her hands on her knees, trying to peer through the loosely nailed sideboards.

"C'mon, they're waiting," Caleb pressed. He could picture a gang of hound dogs springing from under the smokehouse.

"It sounded like it said...*Baby*." Just as Marlee finished speaking, they heard a loud bump come from inside the cabin. "Let's go look in the window."

"Come on, kids!" The urgency in Mr. Patterson's voice made Marlee change her mind and turn away from the smokehouse.

****

The ride in the back of the truck was crowded with Caleb, Marlee, and twenty-five smoked hams. They both sat in silence, holding on to the side of the pickup truck as it bounced over dried tire ruts in the dirt road.

Finally, Marlee spoke. "What do you think it was?"

Caleb shook his head and focused on the trees that seemed to be running past the truck.

"I wish I could have looked in that window," Marlee said.

"Maybe Annabelle had a dog in there. Maybe she has a puppy, and she didn't want the big dogs to hurt it," Caleb reasoned.

"But I heard someone say, *baby*. I know I did. No puppy is gonna say, baby."

"And maybe it barked, you know, the way hound dogs bark." At that, Caleb threw his head back and let out a bawl, trying to make it say *baby*.

"If it sounds like that, it needs to go to the vet!" Marlee squealed, and they both laughed. Caleb let out another "Ba-oh-bee!" They laughed until they had to hold their sides.

Marlee wiped the tears from her eyes with her mitten. "Wonder what that really was?"

Caleb sat quietly for a moment and then turned to Marlee. All the laughter had left his face. "You don't think—"

"Think what?"

"Well, Henry did say...you know."

"Oh, Caleb, Henry's head is about as fat as...as one of these hams."

"I've heard that story in other places, too, not just from Henry. People say strange things happen down there with the creek people. I don't believe what Henry said, but—"

"But nothing! If you believe Annabelle's mama was in that smokehouse, then your head is...well...it's as fat as *all* these hams!"

The truck moved faster now that it was on the paved road, and the two could feel the cold cutting through their shirts and jackets, although the sun was still high above the pines. They pulled their knees close under their chins and turned their coat collars across their cheeks. Leaning on each other, shoulder to shoulder, they didn't speak all the way home.

Chapter 8

Caleb and Marlee jumped out of the truck bed as soon as Mr. Patterson pulled up to the kitchen door of the church.

"Whoa, Caleb! Hold on. We've got to unload these hams." Caleb's dad walked around to the back and released the tailgate.

"But I wanna help put up the wise men and stuff."

"We'll take care of that after we get these hams inside. Now, c'mon." Mr. Austin took a ham by the burlap and gently tossed it to Caleb. "Here ya go!" Caleb stumbled back slightly but caught his balance. He glanced around, but Marlee had already gone inside to help with the decorations.

His dad smiled and gave him a wink. "Good catch."

"Okay. I'm ready!" Caleb pretended to spit in his hands, "Throw me another."

Once they had all the hams inside, Caleb leaned against the doorframe and watched the activity. It was obvious that the women were in charge of the church kitchen. Mrs. Irving, the organist, stood beside Caleb's mother at a long metal table, slicing the hams they had just brought from Smoky Pruitt's place. Some of the ham was to be used for the Christmas social tonight, but most went into baskets to be taken to needy families. Other women scurried around the kitchen, preparing the baskets, adding cheese packets, a box of crackers, and some peppermint sticks. The baskets were then wrapped with green cellophane and set aside with plans to be delivered next week.

Caleb heard Marlee's mother in the social hall area giving directions about where to hang the cutout angels.

Caleb's mother looked up and smiled at Caleb and his dad. "I believe Reverend Anders might need some help finding the nativity figures. We tried to tell him where they were, but I'm not sure he understood."

Mrs. Irving leaned forward and glanced around. "He didn't seem none too happy to go out in that ol' shed," she whispered with a slight giggle.

Caleb and his dad found Preacher Anders at the entrance to the storage shed, broom in hand. "Hello, Reverend." Caleb's dad grinned at Preacher Anders, slinging a broom in the air. He appeared to be fighting one of King Arthur's knights rather than last season's spider webs.

"Oh, hello, Joshua and Caleb. How are y'all on this fine day?"

"Doing good. Need a hand here? Caleb, how 'bout finding the light cord so we can see what we are up against."

"Yes, sir." Caleb climbed over a jumble of folding chairs and located the pull chain that hung from the light fixture.

"I'm not sure what I'm looking for in here. I guess I'm in the right place. The ladies told me that the church puts up a Nativity scene each year and that the parts would be in this shed. It looks as if it hasn't been entered since last Christmas."

At that, Reverend Anders wiped his forehead with a white handkerchief he had retrieved from his pants pocket. His pale complexion and thin body suggested that any of his activities, other than preaching and visiting church members, didn't include physical labor. After moving a few folded tables, two concrete blocks, and a broken lectern, Preacher Anders had perspiration trailing down the side of his face.

"Most of it's right over here." Caleb maneuvered to the far wall where several pieces of plywood leaned. "I helped put them back in here last Christmas."

"Thank you, Caleb," the Reverend said, again pulling his handkerchief from the back pocket of his blue polyester pants.

"We've had these figures all of Caleb's life and then some," Caleb's dad commented. "Ol' Ansel Chapman cut these out in his cabinet shop about fifteen years ago. Then, the art teacher at the high school painted the wise men."

"They both did a first-rate job. They've held up very well indeed," the preacher observed.

"This is my favorite one." Caleb propped up one of the wise men. He looked intently at the colorful figure.

"Ah, that must be Balthazar. Do you know the name of the others?" Reverend Anders asked.

"Um…Casper?" Caleb said, unsure of his answer.

"Well, close, but not spelled like the friendly ghost." the Reverend laughed. "And the other one is Melchior."

The men hefted the larger figures onto their shoulders and carried them to the truck while Caleb brought out the supports and a plywood cutout of a sheep. Reverend Anders leaned against the back of the truck to rest. "You know, we had a live nativity scene at my former church in Asheville."

Caleb wrestled with the sheep but finally laid it into

the truck bed on top of the other figures and turned to the pastor. "Live? How did you do that?"

"Church members signed up for different shifts. They would dress and stand as the characters."

"Did they act it out too?"

"No, they just stood there, but it was a busy road, and traffic lined up, sometimes for miles. It was great for membership, quite an advertisement for the church."

Caleb's dad climbed behind the wheel of the truck. "See y'all in a bit." He drove off to the front of the church, leaving Caleb and Reverend Anders to follow on foot.

"Hey, y'all, wait on me!" Marlee yelled, running out of the side door of the social hall.

"Mary Lee, how are you doing?" Reverend Anders asked, giving her a slight squeeze around the shoulders.

"Just fine. Are y'all going to set up the manger scene now? You know, I always let them use one of my dolls for the baby Jesus. I'll bring it tonight and put it in the manger."

"Preacher Anders said that at his other church, they used to have live people for their manger scene," Caleb said.

"That sounds like fun! Could we do that too?" Marlee asked.

"Well, we're thinking of having a couple of animals out here, just for a few days before Christmas."

"Oh, neat!" Marlee exclaimed. "What kind of animals?"

"Maybe some bears and tigers, you know, the usual." Caleb lightly punched Marlee on the shoulder.

"I'm afraid that might be *bad* for business." The Reverend laughed. "I was talking to Gene Porter. He has a farm and said he could bring a sheep and a goat over for a few days, assuming I could find someone to care for them. Someone would need to get them water and see that they have plenty of hay to eat. Now, I wonder who we could get for the job?" The Reverend glanced down at the kids while he rubbed his chin thoughtfully.

Marlee didn't even look at Caleb. "We'll do it!" she shouted. "Won't we, Caleb?"

"Sure! We can do it during Christmas break."

"Okay, you're hired. Your pay is all the hay you can consume!" The Reverend chuckled at his humor.

"Who knows, we might even dress up one night," Marlee said.

"Oh, no! Please remind me to stay home *that* night," Caleb responded, teasing Marlee.

Marlee playfully stuck her tongue out at Caleb. She turned to the preacher. "Reverend, did y'all use a real baby at your church in Asheville?"

"Usually, no. We considered it one year, but it became too cold, so we reverted to using a doll instead."

"You know Mrs. Rogers, the English teacher? She had a baby last year. Maybe we could ask—"

"I find it best to continue with the tradition of using one of your dolls, don't you agree?" Reverend Anders said, patting Marlee on the shoulder and nodding.

"Yeah, remember last year? It's a good thing we had a doll instead of a real baby out there!" Caleb added.

"Last year? Why, what happened?" the Reverend asked.

"Someone stole my doll! They just took it right outta the manger. Maybe we should tie it down this year."

"Tie down baby Jesus? That can't be right, now can it, Reverend Anders?" Caleb asked.

"I would assume not. Did you ever find out—?"

"But baby Jesus was wrapped up real tight anyways. Why can't we tie him down?" Marlee asked.

"They indeed used swaddling clothes, but I—"

"It was really weird because the doll was right back in the manger Christmas morning," Caleb answered.

"It was? Well, that is rather odd."

"And it stunk to high heavens!" Marlee wrinkled her nose and waved her hand in front of her face. "Mama wouldn't let me keep it. She threw it out on the dump pile. She said it might be germy 'cause it smelled all musty like."

"Yeah, I remember it kinda smelling like—" Caleb didn't finish. His forehead knitted in thought.

****

The social hall at Fletcher First Baptist Church was designed with one purpose in mind: for large numbers of people to gather and eat. The room was big and bright, with fluorescent lights that shone through translucent panels in the ceiling, reflecting the white tile floor and painted concrete walls.

This evening, the hall was changed into a winter scene better than any production the community playhouse could have staged. Mrs. Patterson's Sunday school class had decorated the window sills and support posts with cut garlands of fresh evergreens. Paper snowflakes and angels made by the Girls' Auxiliary hung on the walls. The ladies and their daughters had placed tablecloths on rows of cafeteria tables and arranged sweet-smelling fir boughs as centerpieces.

This was the coldest evening yet. The dark mountains pierced the low gray clouds, and everyone spoke of snow as they scurried in from the parking lot.

"That wind feels like it's comin' down off of ice!" Mrs. Patterson said with a shiver in her voice. She held the door for Caleb and his mother, both carrying casserole dishes.

"Wouldn't it be something if we had a white Christmas this year?" Caleb's mother said.

"Yeah, it's rabbit season, and I could track them in the snow!" Caleb smiled wryly at Marlee.

"Marlee, take this present over and put it under the tree." Mrs. Patterson stopped to smooth one of the white paper table coverings.

"Oh, Mama, do I hav'ta get a present with the other kids this year? I'm not a child anymore."

"I know that, Marlee. But we don't have many children here at our church, and I expect you to set a good example. Now, go on and put that present under the tree."

"Next year, I'll be fifteen, and I'm *not* doin' it!" Marlee, with her hands on her hips, whirled around and stalked over to the Christmas tree.

After Marlee placed her present under the tree, she found Caleb and tugged at his arm. "Let's go put my doll in the manger out front. We saw the lights on when we drove up. I'll get it out of the car."

The two put on their coats and left the social hall. Marlee lifted the doll from the back seat of the car and carefully wrapped it in a blue blanket as if it were a real baby. On their way to the front of the church, they passed Bobby Henderson and his younger sister, Claudia.

"Hey, you two! Sneaking out of church already?" Bobby said with a sneer.

"Just keep walking," Caleb whispered through clenched teeth.

Marlee didn't listen to Caleb. She walked over to Bobby and his sister and showed them her doll. Caleb stood at the edge of the parking lot.

"This is the doll we're using for the baby Jesus in the manger scene."

"So cute!" Claudia said. "Can I hold him?"

Claudia rocked the doll in her arms while Bobby stepped closer to Caleb and laughed. "You and Marlee going to be Mary and Joseph?"

Caleb tensed and squared his shoulders. "Maybe you can be one of the donkeys!"

Claudia and Marlee laughed, but Bobby turned, red-faced, and stormed toward the social hall door. "Come on, Claudia. Let's go inside."

Caleb and Marlee walked to the front of the church. Spotlights shone on the plywood nativity figure. Marlee kneeled and placed her doll into the bed of straw that lined the manger. "I sure hope no one bothers it this year. Maybe when the animals get here, they will protect it."

"I'm getting hungry. Let's go before Bobby eats all the ham and my grandpa's smoked turkey!"

Within the next half-hour, families began arriving in greater numbers. Mrs. Philips, the church pianist, began to play familiar Christmas hymns on the old upright piano. When the ladies entered the social hall, they headed for the tables and placed their covered dishes. They gathered in small groups and shared recipes and holiday plans while the men stood in the parking lot under the streetlight and finished their cigarettes.

To Caleb, one thing was certain at any church gathering: there was enough food for the entire county. He scanned the once-empty tables full of casseroles, pies, and other homemade goodies. At the head of the line of tables were his grandpa's smoked turkeys, carefully sliced and presented in such a display that even the finest chefs would be proud. This year, Caleb considered himself among those chefs. He couldn't wait to start filling his plate with the turkey he helped smoke.

In the corner, the younger children whispered to each other, pointing to the shiny bows and checking the size of each present. They jostled and squirmed for a favored position in front of the Christmas tree, watching wide-eyed as each gift was added to the growing pile under the tree. Later, after the meal and a few words from the pastor, the kids would all draw a number and find their gifts.

On the opposite side of the room from the younger children, Caleb and Marlee found a seat. Albert pulled up a chair next to Caleb, holding a cup of red punch in one hand and a doughnut in the other.

"Hi! What y'all gettin' for Christmas?" he asked, wiping glaze off the corner of his mouth with the sleeve of his white Sunday shirt.

Marlee sat up straight and adjusted her dress. She scanned the room, ignoring Albert's question. "Where's Alice?"

"Oh, squirt's under the tree with the other kids." Albert pointed with his half-eaten doughnut. "So, Caleb, what ya getting' for Christmas?"

Caleb shrugged. "I dunno. How about you?"

"I hope I get a new bike," Albert offered. "One of the red ones I saw at a store over in Asheville. Ever go to Asheville much? They've got the best ice cream shops I've ever seen." He paused and looked around the room, and then turned back to Caleb. "Anyways, what you wantin' for Christmas?"

"I'm hoping for a rifle or maybe a shotgun."

"Boy, I'd love to have one, but my daddy says I'm not old enough, yet. I don't wanna wait two or three more years. But my mama'd have a dying duck fit before she'd let me have a gun right now."

"Good for her. It seems someone has some sense around here!" Marlee broke in. "I don't know why guys think they have to go around shooting animals. It's just plain mean." She threw her head back around so that her blonde curls flew out and came to rest on the shoulder of her Sunday dress.

"Grandpa says hunting actually helps the animals since there's not many more wolves or mountain lions around," Caleb explained.

"I don't see how shooting a poor animal helps it at all. Not at all."

"I heard a bobcat out in the woods the other night. It 'bout scared me half to death. It sounded like a baby cryin', sent chills right up me." Albert shook his whole body for effect and then leaned toward Marlee. "What're you gettin', Marlee?"

But Marlee wasn't listening. She was watching Bobby Henderson and Claudia across the room, laughing with several of their friends. It was obvious to Caleb that she was trying not to notice Albert. He knew that ignoring Albert was like ignoring a fly buzzing around your face. Albert never seemed to recognize obvious hints when someone was tired of talking to him. Kids would fill in seats on the school bus or in the cafeteria just so they wouldn't have to sit with Albert. Caleb and Marlee usually put up with his endless conversations, even though they were irritating.

"Marlee! I said, what ya gettin' for Christmas?" He

repeated louder, this time leaning forward enough to poke her elbow with his finger.

"Uh, I'll be back in a li'l while." Marlee stood and walked across the room toward the Hendersons.

"Where's she goin'?" Albert asked with a mouthful of doughnut.

Caleb didn't answer, only shrugged, but his eyes followed her across the room to where she stood beside Claudia.

"Why's she over there with the snobs?" Albert's thoughts tended to slip out of his mouth as easily as pastries entered.

"They're not snobs; they just have a different upbringing than we do." Caleb stopped. He couldn't believe how much that comment sounded like something his mother would say when, actually, Caleb agreed with Albert.

"Well, call 'em what you want to, but I say they're snobs and the worst kind—church snobs. I mean, if you walked over there right now, Bobby'd start talkin' down to you and stuff. Just because they live out in the country and raise horses don't make 'em any better than you and me." Albert took a large bite of the doughnut as if his observation deserved a reward.

"Maybe so." Caleb remembered last week in Sunday School when Bobby had gone on and on about how his lawyer father would have sued that ol' innkeeper if he had been Joseph's daddy, and how he wouldn't have taken his girl off on a trip with a scrawny donkey. He would have placed her on his prized gelding. Caleb grinned, thinking of his earlier donkey comment.

"Caleb?" Marlee startled him back to the present. "Do you want to go out front to look at the nativity scene?"

"We were just there a little bit ago. Why do you wanna go back?" Caleb looked from Marlee to Albert and then to Bobby, who stood beside Marlee. He sported a conceited smirk as proudly as his yellow alpaca sweater, flawlessly pressed pants, and spit-shined penny loafer shoes.

"C'mon, Bobby, let's go see the baby Jesus." Claudia pulled Bobby's arm, and the three started for the social hall door. Marlee paused and looked over her shoulder at Caleb and Albert, still sitting in the folding chairs.

"You coming, Caleb?"

"Attention, please! May I have everyone's attention!" The youth director, Mrs. Preston, tapped a spoon on a water glass several times. "I want to thank everyone for coming tonight and bringing this wonderful food. Before we say our blessing, I want to remind all the young people that we'll be going to the Cedar Hills Children's Home next Saturday to have a Christmas party for the children there. Everyone needs to bring a wrapped gift for a boy or a girl. I have some mimeographed sheets on the back table that will give you more information. Please be sure to pick one up before you leave tonight. Now, I'll turn it over to Reverend Anders."

"Thank you, Julia. I want to thank everyone responsible for these exquisite decorations and the delectable cuisine. Let us thank the Lord for his bounty. At this time, I will ask one of our dear senior members to lead us in prayer. Jeremiah Austin, would you bless the food for us?"

Grandpa straightened his back and nodded to

Reverend Anders. "Let us pray."

"I hope you're not hungry," Caleb teased, leaning toward Albert. Caleb's grandpa was a man of very few words in a group unless he was praying. He would clasp his hands across his belly, point his face toward heaven, and, with closed eyes, forget that anyone existed but him and the Lord.

****

"Dear Lord, we come to Thee at this special time of year, a time for love, a time for fellowship with friends and family, and most of all, a time to worship Thee, the Giver of all Life."

Caleb sat still in his chair beside Albert. He peeked out of one eye. Where were Marlee and the Hendersons? Surely, they hadn't gone outside when dinner was about to start. Right then, he spotted them by the door.

"We come to Thee, oh Lord, with humble hearts. Our hearts are forever thankful for Thy bounty, not only for the physical goodness You have provided us but for Thou merciful grace that showers down from heaven, grace so undeserved. Forgive us, oh Lord, for our many shortcomings."

Albert had his eyes shut so tightly that little wrinkles radiated out from the sockets. With his head still bowed, Caleb peered across his right shoulder and spotted Marlee now sitting next to Bobby in a line of folding chairs by the door. Stephen Satterfield, Bobby's friend, sat on the other side of Marlee. All three of them whispered to each other. Stephen poked Bobby in the ribs across Marlee's lap and pointed across the room in Caleb's direction.

"Forgive us, almighty God, of our sins. Forgive our sins of omission as well as those of commission. Bless

this church, oh Lord, this body of believers, as we make our way in the world. Help us, oh Lord, to be a lighthouse showing the way through the darkness and to never place our light under a basket, but to let your light shine through us for all to see."

Caleb was incredulous. "I can't believe it! Poking and giggling during my grandpa's blessing! I knew that ol' Bobby Henderson was no good!"

"Lord, we thank you for the gift of your son, Jesus, who you sent to this world so that we might be saved."

Caleb then glanced at Albert, hoping for a witness to this blasphemy, but Albert still had his eyes shut tight, and his face grimaced like he was thinking about a hard arithmetic problem. Caleb shot a look back across the room. Now Marlee was sitting with her hands folded in her lap and her eyes closed.

"Boy, I bet she'll let them have it when Grandpa finishes praying because she really likes my grandpa and can't stand misbehaving in church. They're in for a tongue-lashing for sure!" Caleb smiled at the thought.

At that moment, Bobby stuck his finger in Marlee's ribs, and she let out a slight squeal. She slapped her hand over her mouth, but instead of cutting him in half with a sharp gaze, as Caleb expected, she playfully smacked him on the arm and closed her eyes. But her mouth still wore a silly grin.

"Help us to keep the spirit of Christmas and to extend a hand of generosity to the less fortunate, not only at this time of year but in the seasons to come."

Caleb turned back and shut his eyes as tightly as Albert's. "Grinning during my grandpa's prayer! And he was poking her ribs right here in church! I oughta go right over there and give him back his black eye!" Caleb thought as he gritted his teeth.

"And, Lord, thank you for the hands that prepared this meal, this plentiful harvest of which we shall partake. Bless it, oh Lord, to the nourishment of our bodies so that we might have the strength to do Your will. It is in the name of Jesus Christ, our Lord and Savior. Amen."

"C'mon!" Albert bolted from his seat and headed for the serving line. Caleb reluctantly followed, torn between looking at Marlee and Bobby or ignoring them. As they waited in line behind Albert's sister and several other children, Caleb casually glanced toward the chairs. The empty chairs. The side door was just then closing shut.

"Where's Marlee?" Albert asked, picking up his knife and fork from the steel tray. "She's gonna miss out. The line's gettin' long."

Caleb shrugged. "That's her problem."

They continued through the line, Caleb watching as Albert strategically placed food so that he could stack two helpings onto one plate. "You'd better get it while ya can; there might not be any seconds!" said Albert. He looked over at Caleb's half-full plate. "I must be a lot hungrier than you."

True, Caleb wasn't as hungry as he was a while ago. When he got to his grandpa's smoked turkey, he didn't even feel like taking a slice, but he did. After all, he had helped cook it.

"So, ya think ya might get a rifle for Christmas?" Albert asked while waiting for his sister to finish dipping the macaroni and cheese. "I sure hope I don't get any underwear. I always get lots of underwear."

"I hope I don't get any penny loafers!" Caleb

responded, almost to himself.

"Oh, boy! Banana puddin'! That's my favorite!" Albert grabbed his plate and hurried toward the dessert table.

Just as Caleb was almost at the end of the serving line, he felt a strong tug on his arm. He turned to face Marlee. Her eyes were wide, and her face pale.

"Caleb! You gotta come see!" My doll! It's gone!

Chapter 9

The brass bell jingled when Caleb and Marlee entered Harper's General Store. The clink of the old bell always ushered in memories for Caleb of his early childhood when he had come to Harper's with his daddy. The wooden shelves and tables had seemed full of treasures, and the glass candy case had been a fantasyland for a four year old. Caleb had always left with a licorice string dangling from his mouth.

It seemed that no matter how much the world outside changed, Harper's Store remained the same. The barrels of nails in the hardware section might have held newer nails, but the old metal scale for weighing them still hung, timeless, like the pendulum of a grandfather's clock. Mr. Harper never seemed to change either. He could usually be found sitting behind the counter reading the morning paper or maybe standing on his tiptoes tending the wall of dry goods with a feather duster, wearing his denim apron and white shirt fastened to the last button. Even his greeting remained unchanged in all the years Caleb could remember.

"Howdy, partner!" the old gentleman sang out.

"Hi, Mr. Harper." Caleb walked over to the counter where the elderly man stood. Through all the sameness of Harper's Store, one change was obvious. Caleb now stood as tall as this small, thin man with wire-rimmed glasses.

"And hello, pretty lady. What can I do for you two?"

Marlee placed her hands on the counter. "We came to get some presents for the kids at Cedar Hills Children's Home."

"Looking for anything in particular?"

"No, we're not sure what we want yet," Marlee said.

"I got in a new shipment of toys last week. You might want to take a look at 'em." Mr. Harper pointed the handle of the feather duster towards the front shelves.

The first thing Marlee saw was the baby doll dressed in a nightgown. She cradled it in her arms and rocked back and forth. "Why would anybody want to steal my li'l baby doll from a church? When Bobby and I saw my baby Jesus gone from the manger the other night, I almost had a fit right there in front of him. Stealing's not right, especially at church!"

At the mention of Bobby's name, Caleb's chest tightened. A wave of irritation flooded him as he thought of Marlee and Bobby together at the church social. But he couldn't stay mad at Marlee. After all, she was his best friend. And last Saturday night, when she had discovered her baby doll missing from the church nativity scene, Caleb had been the first person she had run to tell. That made him feel a bit better, but Caleb could feel his insides twist into a knot when she talked about Bobby Henderson and how he wanted her to come to his house and ride horses with him and Claudia.

Caleb turned to Marlee. "Did you ever think that maybe Bobby did it?"

"Bobby? Do you think Bobby took my doll? That's crazy!"

"Well, he did see us carryin' it around the front of the church to the manger that night. Sounds like

91

somethin' he'd do."

"You're just still mad at him about Halloween night. I'm sure he had nothing to do with taking my doll. Anyway, let's forget about Bobby."

Caleb wished he could.

Marlee turned her attention to the toy rack. "Maybe I'll get this baby doll for one of the little girls. I think I have enough money." She turned the doll over and looked for the price tag while Caleb browsed through the baseball gloves.

Just then, the brass bell jingled. A sound of boots clomped unevenly across the old wooden floorboards.

Marlee leaned close to Caleb and poked him in his side. "It's Smoky Pruitt!" she whispered.

Smoky limped to the counter and growled his request, interrupting Mr. Harper's greeting.

"Well, hello there, Mr. Pru—"

"I need some fence staples. How much are they?" He didn't browse or talk about the weather like most men. He appeared to be in a hurry.

"Ah, mending a fence. There's always something to do around a place," Mr. Harper said. He seemed ready to strike up a conversation.

"Got any?" Barked Smoky. His brow furrowed, and his fingers drummed the counter impatiently.

"Oh, sure thing, right over here." Caleb watched as Smoky and Mr. Harper walked to the back of the store. Marlee tugged on Caleb's shirt.

"Let's look and see if Annabelle came with him."

"Well, she didn't come in, so I guess—"

"Remember, she said she sits in the truck when they come to Harper's. C'mon." Marlee walked to the front window and looked at the graveled parking area. Caleb followed reluctantly behind, slapping his fist into the new baseball glove he was holding and glancing over his shoulder at Smoky and Mr. Harper.

When they saw Annabelle sitting in the truck, Marlee turned immediately and went to the candy case by the cash register.

"Did you decide on a gift, young lady?" Mr. Harper asked, leaving Smoky Pruitt in the hardware area.

"I'm going to look some more in a little bit, but first, I'd like a stick of peppermint candy." Marlee laid a coin on the counter. Mr. Harper handed her the red and white stick wrapped in a paper napkin.

She turned and headed straight for the door. "Let's go outside and see Annabelle for a minute."

Caleb laid the glove back on the table and hesitantly followed Marlee. He gave another quick look at Smoky as the brass bell jingled, and then the door closed behind them.

They could see Annabelle through the truck window with her head down. Her hair covered most of her face. When they walked up to the old truck, Marlee tapped on the glass. Annabelle didn't look up. She sat staring at the only button on her coat, rubbing it like she was polishing a prized medallion. The old gray coat was frayed at the cuffs and hem and appeared too small for the girl.

"I don't think she wants to talk. Let's go back inside. We need to pick out our presents," Caleb insisted. He turned back toward the store.

"Oh, she's just being shy." Marlee reached for the handle on the truck and, with some force, twisted it so the dented door opened with a loud creak. Annabelle started at Marlee's intrusion.

"Hi, Annabelle, how're you doing?"

The girl didn't respond but instead glanced nervously from the store window to Caleb and then to Marlee.

"So, why don't you come into the store? Mr. Harper has lots of nice things today."

"My daddy told me ta wait here."

"Why can't you come in, just for a minute?"

"Marlee, if Smo—I mean her daddy don't—" Marlee's hand waving behind her back cut Caleb's words short. He turned away, picked up a handful of gravel, and began to toss the rocks at a stop sign across the street. He didn't want to be a part of Marlee's plan but felt the need to stay close just in case Smoky returned to the truck.

"Here, I brought you something." Marlee held out the candy stick wrapped in the napkin. Caleb stopped throwing and waited to see what Annabelle would do.

Annabelle looked at the candy and then directly into Marlee's eyes. "Why ya givin' that stick candy ta me?"

"I thought you might like it. Here, you can have it."

Annabelle's eyes remained fixed on the candy, but her hands still rubbed the button on her coat.

"I want you to have it. I got it just for you." Marlee slowly reached, took the girl's small hand, and placed the wrapped candy stick into her dirty palm. "Here, it's yours," Marlee said, closing Annabelle's fingers around the peppermint stick.

The small girl held the candy tightly in her hand. "Thank ya, kindly," said Annabelle, still looking at the candy stick. Then she opened the napkin, broke the stick in half, and held a piece out for Marlee.

"Why, thank you, Annabelle, that's mighty sweet of you." Marlee took the candy and gave it a lick. "Um, I like peppermint." Marlee licked the candy as she turned and smiled at Caleb. The look of victory shone in her eyes.

Annabelle took her half of the stick and broke it again. She carefully wrapped one of the pieces in the paper napkin and shoved it deep into her coat pocket. She smiled at Marlee while licking the other stick.

"Do you always go places with your daddy?" Marlee asked.

Annabelle licked her lips. "Sometimes I hav' ta stay home an' watch after...thangs."

"Oh, like your hound dogs and pigs?"

"I slop the pigs ev'r mornin' an' night. I feed th' dogs too." Annabelle's bright eyes danced as she spoke.

"Do your dogs have names?"

"We...uh, I named 'em. Lemme see, there's Howler an' Blackie an'—"

"Where'd ya git that!" Smoky boomed as he jerked the truck door open. Marlee jumped back like someone had hit her. She hadn't heard the bell jingle on Harper's door. With widened eyes, she quickly searched around for Caleb. He was standing right behind her, fear written across his face.

"I said, where'd ya git that candy?" Smoky's right fist was clenched so tightly that the bony knuckles were white. With his other hand, he snatched the stick from Annabelle. The little girl cast her eyes down and rubbed the button of her coat.

"Um...Mr. Pruitt, I gave it to her," Marlee confessed.

"Well, take it back. We don't need no charity." He thrust the wet stick through the open door at Marlee.

Marlee didn't move. She looked through the truck

window at Annabelle, who had buried her cheek into the coat collar.

Caleb tugged at Marlee's coat. "C'mon, Marlee. We better be—."

Caleb couldn't believe what Marlee said next. "Mr. Pruitt, I'm sorry. But I wanted her to have it. Annabelle's my friend. We were just talking…about her dogs and stuff." Marlee's voice cracked, and her eyes welled up with tears.

Caleb braced himself, expecting them to be told to "git" just like the dogs under the porch. But instead, for a long moment, nothing happened. Smoky stared out the windshield, looking beyond the children and Harper's Store. It was as if he was gazing at something far away, past the cedar hedgerow and pasture behind the store.

No one moved.

Smoky's stern features began to soften, and he finally turned back to his daughter. He took his finger, gently wiped a drip of red candy from the corner of Annabelle's mouth, and then placed the stick back in her hand.

"We best be goin' now." Smoky reached and closed the door as Marlee and Caleb backed away from the truck. Annabelle held the peppermint stick up. The little girl stared at Marlee until the old truck turned out of sight.

Chapter 10

Riding a bus was always an adventure for Caleb, so long as it wasn't to and from school. Piling into a Henderson County yellow school bus with forty other kids, all armed with books and lunch boxes, was a necessity that some children had to endure. Fortunately, Caleb and Marlee lived a short stretch from the school, a journey they braved on foot, regardless of the weather. So, a bus ride to school was a hardship they never had to endure. However, this outing to the Cedar Hills Children's Home was on a Saturday, and less than half of the church bus seats were filled with the youth group. Caleb was far from excited about today's trip, especially since Marlee had walked to the back of the bus to sit with Bobby Henderson and his cronies. Caleb glared out of the bus window at the ghost-like clouds floating across the mountain ridges.

"Where's she goin'?" Albert asked, leaning over the cracked vinyl seat where Caleb and Marlee had been sitting. Caleb knew Albert didn't care why Marlee left; he just wanted her seat. A definite seating pattern always emerged on the bus. No one ever planned or talked about it, but each knew where to sit. The elementary kids sat in the front of the bus, and the more popular older youth took up the rear. Everyone else occupied the middle section. Albert usually sat by himself.

"Why'd she go back there with them?" Albert slid

in beside Caleb. "We weren't talkin' 'bout huntin' or killin' animals or nothin' gross."

Caleb shrugged and continued to look out the window at the cold afternoon rain. The gray mist, along with the smoke from the hillside houses, draped a gloomy blanket across the countryside. This blanket had spread across Caleb's mood.

It had been several years since Caleb had been to the Cedar Hills Home with his church group, and it was taking far longer than he had remembered. He passed the time absently commenting on Albert's observations about anything from hunting dogs to motorbikes while, at the same time, he tried to ignore the periodic roar of laughter from the rear of the bus. He also tried to ignore the knot in his stomach.

The bus drove over a bridge, and Caleb noticed the river below, meandering through the mountainside. He focused on the sandy edges of the waterway, and in his mind, saw Marlee and Bobby walking along the bank.

In his daydream, the water suddenly swirled, and from within its murky depths, the creature appeared. Marlee screamed as the amphibious man-like monster approached the bank with its arms outstretched and its mouth gaping with chisel-like teeth. Bobby stood still, paralyzed with fear, as Marlee screamed for help. The brush behind them seemed to explode as the white stallion Caleb was riding crashed through the bushes and came to a halt beside the frightened children.

The monster was on the bank now, only a few feet from Marlee.

Caleb jumped down from his steed and stood between the monster and Marlee.

"Get on the horse, both of you, and ride to safety!"

Caleb cried.

"But Caleb, what about you?" Marlee screamed.

"I'll be all right. Just do as I say. Now!" As Marlee and Bobby rode to the crest of the hill, Caleb brandished a sword and fought the creature with a fury, eventually sending him back to his watery tomb.

"Oh, Caleb, you're so brave!" Marlee sighed, throwing her arms around his neck.

"Well? Have ya?" Albert poked Caleb in the ribs, bringing him back. "Have ya ever been fly fishin'?"

"Uh, no, I've just been regular fishing," Caleb said. "Why?"

"I just heard Bobby telling some story 'bout fly fishin' for salmon in Alaska. That guy really thinks he's somethin', ya know?"

Caleb turned to the window and caught the last glimpses of the river in the valley below.

"Yeah, he must be."

****

The bus pulled in front of the Cedar Hills Children's Home. The old house was smaller than Caleb had remembered, but he was just a kid the last time he was there.

Mrs. Preston told them the history last Sunday in Sunday School. The previous owners who lived in the house kept foster children. Eventually, the family donated the house and land to the county, and it has been operating as a home for children ever since. Mrs. Preston told them about a big fire five years ago on Christmas Eve. Wood heat was all that was available at the time, and a child had gotten too close to the fireplace. When her gown caught fire, she ran screaming, spreading the flames to the Christmas tree and drapes. The child hadn't been burned too badly, but because of this accident, the state put enough money into the home to update the heating system and build a large activity room. "All things work for good when we love the Lord." Mrs. Preston had clutched her Bible tightly after telling the story.

The activity area had the feeling of a large living room. On the tile floor lay a square of tattered blue carpet bordered by several couches and chairs, all needing repair. Duct tape covered some of the holes in the fabric, but the cotton filling spilled out from other worn spots. Game tables with checkers, chess, and Parcheesi boards lined one wall. An upright piano stood framed against the opposite wall, directly under a painting of Jesus praying in the garden of Gethsemane.

Beside the piano, a cedar Christmas tree stood. There were no lights on the tree, and small, hand-made construction paper decorations of glue and glitter hung from the branches.

"Children, children, may I have your attention, please?" Mrs. Williams, the home administrator, clapped her hands with a resounding crack. She must have been an elementary teacher at some time, Caleb smirked.

Mrs. Williams turned to the twenty-three residents, all bunched together at one end of the room. They ranged in age from about four to the early teens.

"Children, I want you to welcome Mrs. Preston and the youth group from Fletcher First Baptist Church. She's brought a group of her young people, and they've planned a party for us. Isn't that exciting?" Several of the younger residents clapped their hands and jumped up and down. The older kids never looked directly at the visitors. They shuffled their feet and stared at the floor.

During the next hour, Mrs. Williams played the out-of-tune piano as the children sang Christmas carols, played games, and ate the snacks brought by the church. One particular boy, Andrew, had found himself at home in Marlee's lap. He was about six years old but smaller than most other children his age. He didn't talk much or demand attention; he simply smiled and snuggled close to his new friend.

"What's your favorite game?" Marlee asked the boy while he munched on a large sugar cookie shaped like an angel. Andrew shrugged and stuffed another bite of cookie into his mouth.

"I bet you like baseball." Caleb walked up and bent down in front of Marlee and Andrew. Finally. One opportunity to be with Marlee without Bobby nearby.

"You know, you remind me of someone I know who lives in my town. She doesn't talk much either." Marlee wrapped her arms around the boy. "Do you have any brothers or sisters here, Andrew?"

"I had a baby brother. But he died."

Marlee's eyes met Caleb's. Her mouth opened slightly, but no words came out. It was rare for Marlee to be at a loss for words, but Caleb recognized her helpless expression and came to the rescue. "Hey, Andrew. I bet when it snows, y'all go sledding down that big hill in front of the house." Andrew turned to Caleb, his eyes as big as saucers.

"Yeah! Last year, we sledded on th' eatin' trays. I went fast!" He threw his hands out like they were sledding on the snow, spilling cookie crumbs in Marlee's lap.

"Oh, I bet that was fun!" Marlee let loose a boisterous laugh.

"Children! Attention, please!" Mrs. Williams said, standing by the Christmas tree. "Everyone, come over here, and we'll give out the wonderful presents our guests have brought. Now, Mrs. Preston will pass out some numbers on pink paper for the girls and blue paper for the boys."

Caleb kept his eye on the ball and the glove he had brought. Maybe Andrew would get his gift. He hoped so. But after a few minutes of calling numbers and handing out gifts, he saw the prized gift go to a nine-year-old boy named Michael. When Michael opened his present, he held the glove high above his head and beamed a broad smile. Caleb made his way over to the boy and spent the next twenty minutes with him against the far wall, playing a light game of catch.

In the meantime, Marlee joined a make-believe tea party in the middle of the blue rug. A four-year-old girl named Debbie cuddled the doll Marlee had brought, and they were helping another girl play with her new tea set.

On the other side of the room, most of the small boys had, by now, crowded around Bobby Henderson, watching wide-eyed as he demonstrated his yo-yo skills. "This is called walking the dog," Bobby said, loud enough for everyone to hear. He ran his yo-yo along the floor, and the crowd clapped. Bobby grinned and rewound his yo-yo.

"Show me how to do that!" A ten-year-old pushed forward. He had chosen Bobby's gift, and since no one had a yo-yo at Cedar Hills, he was the envy of the other boys.

"You're not ready for that yet." Bobby turned his back on the boy. "Now, here's rockin' the cradle." Bobby showed the trick to the other children.

Bobby's tricks caught Michael's attention from across the room. He tossed the new glove onto the floor and ran to the group. Alone, Caleb picked up the ball and glove and walked to a table in the middle of the room where the coloring book and crayon set that Albert had brought had also been abandoned. He plopped into a chair and tried to ignore the attention surrounding Bobby Henderson across the room.

"Can I try?" Andrew asked, reaching out to Bobby. "Please?"

"Well, okay," Bobby said, handing Andrew his yo-yo. "But be careful, this one is mine, and it's *real* expensive."

Now, almost everyone was around Bobby, except for the tea party girls and a few teenagers playing cards in the corner.

Marlee bent down and slipped the yo-yo string on Andrew's finger. The boy's arm went up, and he slung the yo-yo toward the floor as he had seen Bobby do. The red wheel followed the string and crashed on the hard tile floor, bursting the spinning toy. The children gasped and then roared with laughter.

"You idiot, that's my best yo-yo!" Bobby screamed, his face red. He pointed to where the toy had spun out of sight. "You've probably broken it for good! Now go find it!"

Stunned, Andrew shrank backward and ran after the broken pieces of the yo-yo. He fell to his knees, looking under the tables and chairs. But Albert had already picked up the pieces.

"Here, lemme show you; it's easy ta fix," Albert said, bending down in front of Andrew. The string was still dangling from the little boy's hand. "Now you can take it back to Bobby."

"Is it broke?" Andrew's voice cracked. Tears filled his eyes.

Just then, Marlee slipped the string off Andrew's finger. "No, it's fine. But let me take it back to him, okay?" Her lips tightened while she rapidly wound the loose string around the yo-yo and looked up at Albert.

"Thank you for fixing it, Albert. That was very sweet."

"Oh, well, it was…I mean…I have one and…um." Albert shuffled his feet and stuck his hands deep into his blue jeans pockets. "C'mon, Andrew, let's go finish colorin' Mickey Mouse."

Marlee held the expensive yo-yo out in front of her like a smelly, dead rat and marched over to the snack table where Bobby Henderson lounged against the wall, munching loudly on potato chips and laughing with Stephen and Claudia.

Caleb sat with Albert and Andrew around the coloring table, but kept his eyes on Marlee when she approached Bobby. He had seen that strong-minded expression and determined walk before. He smiled, knowing that Bobby was about to get an earful

Marlee stopped in front of Bobby. "Here!" She was still holding the yo-yo out at arm's length.

Bobby took it from her and inspected it, turning it over and over in his hand. "Well, it looks all right. I'll try it out in a minute. Tell ol' Albert thanks for me."

"Tell him yourself! That was so mean the way you talked to Andrew! Marlee whirled around and stalked swiftly to the other side of the room with both hands bound into tight fists.

****

The bus rattled down the hill into the dark, mountain night. Fog obscured most of the landscape except for an occasional dim light from a house embedded in the hillside. Marlee unfolded the picture Andrew gave her of Goofy riding a bicycle. An occasional headlight from a car allowed her to see the blues, reds, and greens Andrew had used to color his picture. She had returned to her seat with Caleb while Albert leaned over the back to talk to them.

Marlee held up the drawing. "You know, he seemed to have more fun coloring this page for me than he did anything else," Marlee said, breaking the silence.

"Yeah," Albert added. "His favorite color is blue. He told me that."

Marlee turned toward the window. She fell silent and leaned her head against the rattling pane. Caleb could see Marlee's reflection on the glass, superimposed on the dark countryside beyond. They passed a cluster of small shacks buried deep into the hills. A shimmer of yellow light reached through one of the windows into the dark hemlock forest. Marlee turned to Caleb.

"Wonder if Annabelle would like living here? At Cedar Hills, I mean."

Caleb didn't answer. He looked around the bus at the young kids in the front and then at Bobby and his friends in the back, where they sat, silent.

He had no idea if Annabelle would enjoy living at the Children's Home. He was just glad to have his old friend back.

Chapter 11

The smell of turnip greens cooking in a slab of fatback spread throughout his grandparents' kitchen. Caleb heard the knife crack on the cutting board before he saw Mattie sitting on her stool, chopping vegetables and humming Amazing Grace.

All of Caleb's life, Mattie had helped his grandmother with cooking and light housework. Caleb stopped by after school to see Mattie about as much as he did to see his grandparents. And Mattie always made him feel like she was waiting for him to come and visit. Most of the time, he would find her hovering over a steaming pot of turnip greens or carefully polishing the dining room furniture as if she had just bought it and had it delivered to her own home. Her voice, seasoned from her Gullah childhood on the Carolina Sea islands, had a musical quality, a cadence to her words. Caleb often wondered if all Negro women's words were as cheerful as hers and if they all talked about God and heaven.

"Well, young Caleb, what you doin' here so early?" Mattie handed Caleb a piece of chopped carrot.

"It's Christmas vacation, so we got out of school a little early." He scooted a stool next to Mattie and sat by the warm stove. Her long cotton dress was loose and flowed across her ample body to the floor like the matriarch in one of the stories she liked to tell Caleb.

Mattie stirred the greens and noticed Caleb watching

the spoon make circles in the steaming pot.

"Ah, yes, I 'member Christmas when I was a wee girl on th' island. It be such a magical time, even if we didn't have much. There's just somethin' about th' air this time of year. Ev'n smell differ'nt, you know? "Mattie stopped stirring and beat the spoon on the pot rim. She laid it in the tray and looked at Caleb. He didn't seem to be listening to her.

"Somethin' hangin' on your mind, young man?"

With a mouthful of carrots, Caleb hesitated, "Mattie, were you poor when you were little?"

"Child, when th' Lord be in your heart, you have riches you don't ev'n know 'bout." Mattie held her hands as if she was reaching toward heaven.

Caleb wasn't sure what to say. Between his family, church, and Mattie, he knew about heavenly riches. Yet, people were still poor. He often wondered if they knew they were different from other folks. Didn't they know that they were not like other people? He took a bite of his carrot and let his eyes follow Mattie's gaze to the ceiling. She glanced down at Caleb, smiling.

"But, guess dat's not what you be talkin' about, now is it?"

"No, ma'am."

She looked across the room through the window as if she were searching for something in the woods beyond.

"After my daddy passed, my mama and th' rest of us done gone to live with my aunt in Georgia. I was 'bout eleven, I guess. That's when I found out jus' how dirt po we *really* was. Why, our flapjacks be so thin they only had one side!" Mattie let loose a hearty laugh and slapped her knee.

"What happened in Georgia?"

"On th' island, we use to grow everthin'. Never ran outta nothin' 'cause we had a fine garden. And vegetables, child, we growed ever kind you could put a name to. And if we didn't have it, a neighbor would. On the island, ever'body shared ever'thin'. Then we moved to Brunswick, Georgia, an' lived in a small house in town. I mean it be so small when we was all inside, a bug couldn't even fly in!" Mattie threw her head back and let out a rush of laughter.

"Did you ever go back? To the island, I mean?"

"No, see, there be this little thing what the Good Book call pride. An' my mama, she had more than her share of that. It was my daddy don grew up on the island, so Mama felt like she needed to be with her people after my daddy passed."

"How did your daddy die?"

"He just get way down. Some say it was from a snake, an' some say a root was put on him. I don't rightly know."

Caleb wondered if he should even ask anything else. He had heard her mention the root several times. Sometimes, she called it the hoo-doo. But when she talked about the root, she would lower her voice and speak reverently. The old stories about the conjure men on the island fascinated him, but hearing talk about that stuff scared him a little, too.

"You believe in that stuff, Mattie?"

"Well, I've seen some strange things. But, like I was sayin', if the folks thought it was the root, then they was afraid of my mama an' all us chil'en. That's partly why we left to Georgia."

"Do the people on the island still believe in the

root?"

Mattie picked up her spoon and stirred the pot. She handed the spoon to Caleb. He began to stir while Mattie walked to a small table across the room where a pile of towels, fresh from the clothesline, had been tossed.

"I don hav' no mind to what they think. I was only a young'un when we left."

"You ever see anybody do any of…it? When you were a little girl, I mean?"

"Oh, our house been painted blue."

"What did that do?"

"They say it' s'pose to keep th' haints an' hags away, an' I guess 'cause I never seen no haints, it be workin' right fine!" Mattie let loose another hearty laugh that shook her body from head to foot. "But my daddy never really did give up the root, or so say stories I've heard about 'em."

"Tell me one. Tell me a story about your daddy," Caleb pleaded.

"Oh, child, your grandma gonna think all I be doin' 'round here is run my mouth."

"Please? I love your stories, Mattie." He knew Mattie loved storytelling about as much as she loved singing, so he didn't have to beg too much.

"Well, you let me pour the water outta those greens, and then you keep these beans from scorchin', and I'll tell you about my Aunt Chi-Chi."

"Is this the aunt you moved in with in Georgia?"

"No, no. Chi-Chi was ma daddy's li'l sister. She be bury before I was born. Her name was Chinue." Mattie bowed her head as if she was going to pray. "It mean God's Own Blessin'. Anyways, ever'one in the village just name her Chi-Chi."

Caleb stirred the beans. He looked intently at Mattie. "So, Chi-Chi lived on the island?"

"A li'l while, but they say she had a spirit. She be a seer."

"A what?"

"Chi-Chi was special to th' island folk because she be birthed with th' veil. That was suppose—"

"The veil. That sounds like Annabelle Pruitt," Caleb interrupted.

"—to give her—" Mattie paused, sat up straight, and cut her eyes at Caleb. "What you say about th' Pruitt girl?"

"She's Smoky Pruitt's daughter. Marlee and I come across her a time or two. Marlee's got it in her head that she can help Annabelle somehow. Maybe become her friend."

Mattie shook her head. "That child don't need no help. She be born with th' veil, too. I sawed it. I was th' one don birthed her.

"That's what my mamma told me. So, what's so important about the veil?"

"There's a diff'rnce. Depends where you be." Mattie pulled a dust cloth from a deep pocket in the folds of her skirt and slowly wiped the kitchen hutch as she talked. "On th' island, Chi-Chi was a blessin'. Folks always bringin' their babies for her to touch. Thought it would protect them from th' spirits, an' such. People 'round here prob'ly see that sort of thing like a curse." Mattie sat on her stool and turned toward Caleb, "Anyhow, Chi-Chi wanted to do good things for her people, but she figur'd she'd have to find out about th' rest of th' world 'fore she could help 'em much."

"So, she left the island?" Caleb asked. "Where'd she

go?"

"Soon as she hold up th' money to buy a ferry ticket to Beaufort, off she went. Why, she be only sixteen years ol', but she sold baskets to th' white folks who came over to th' island. That's th' way she got money for th' ferry boat, and maybe a meal or two. Yeah, always had the long eye across the water."

Caleb nodded as if he understood.

"But my daddy say th' folks across th' water didn't have nothin' we needed.

"So, off she go. Somehow, she got to know a family in Beaufort who needed a housegirl. You know, somebody to live there an' help out with th' chores. She'd send letters home every once in a while, tellin' my daddy what things was like. They say he didn't like it, none too good. Tried to git her to come on home a time o' two, but she don set her mind. You see, child, she always be looking for somethin' bigger across the water."

Mattie told the story to Caleb with her whole body. With hands waving in the air and her eyes as big as the saucers on the dining table, Mattie made Chi-Chi's story come alive.

****

The antebellum-style home overlooking the Beaufort County marshlands was not a mansion to most, but to Chi-Chi it might as well have a pearl gate and paths of gold. The property that had once served as a small working rice plantation was now down to only about five acres, mostly of woodlands and marsh. The Hampton family owned it, and there was still a good bit of old money circulating through the relatives, enough to keep the status of South Carolina Lowcountry bluebloods.

Chi-Chi had been hired by Ellen Hampton to clean and cook for her and her husband, Marion, in exchange for a small wage, leftovers, and a servant's cottage out back of the house. Christmas was only a week away, and the chores seemed to have tripled with decorating and preparing for the arrival of Edward, Ellen, and Marion's son.

It was December 1943, and Edward had been wounded in the army while serving in Europe, so he was being discharged. A full recovery was expected, and with the help of a few well-placed letters to the right congressmen, Marion was able to have him home before Christmas.

"Una want da vines in here, Ma'am?" Chi-Chi held the freshly cut greenery in both hands across the top of her apron to keep it from dragging on the parlor's Persian rug.

"That's English ivy, Chi-Chi. You can just drape it across the mantle but don't knock off any of my china. It was given to me by my great-grandmother," Mrs. Hampton cautioned sternly.

"Yes'um." Chi-Chi began carefully weaving the ivy between the china and the pictures of Edward spread across the marble mantelpiece. She took her dust rag and polished the brass picture frames before returning to the kitchen to check on the turkey roasting in the oven.

Chi-Chi loved taking care of the house. She often pretended she lived there and that the Hamptons were her dinner guests. When no one was around, she sat at the antique dining table and ran her hands across the petit point seat covers. She would fix a place setting of the fine china and pretend to be entertaining guests as she had seen Mrs. Hampton do so often. She would take one of the decorative folding fans, gently wave the hand-painted magnolia blossom below her chin, and ask her imaginary guests if all was well.

Occasionally, she dreamed that Edward and Ellen Hampton had adopted her. In her imagination, she would be dressed in frilly, clean white dresses with neat, straight sashes and bows tied in the back. They addressed her as their "darling Chinue" rather than "Chi-Chi." Edward and Ellen would dote on her, smiling and listening intently to her every word.

But this was the fantasy of a young girl.

In reality, Chi-Chi lived behind the house in a one-room brick cottage with no running water and only a fireplace for heat. Although she cooked all of the meals, she was never allowed the privilege of eating at the Hamptons' table, and she could only eat in the kitchen when the company wasn't around. Otherwise, she had to eat in her cottage.

"Chi-Chi, do you remember everything we need to have ready for tomorrow? Edward will come before noon, and the guests will arrive by eleven o'clock." Mrs. Hampton flitted around the kitchen, checking the tablecloth, polished silver, and the candles.

"I 'member evertin' what been tell to me, ma'am."

"You know the linen napkins should be washed and folded properly and the candles trimmed. I don't want any wax on the tablecloth."

"Yes'um, I bina seein for dat."

"And you'll need to polish the furniture in the dining room. And, of course, make sure the parsley is fresh. I *hate* wilted garnishes."

"Yes'um, I be knowin' all you don told to me." Chi-

Chi finished basting the turkey and slid it back into the oven. Mrs. Hampton said something about hand towels and strode off down the hall.

By the time she was dismissed, it was way past nightfall, and Chi-Chi was exhausted. She adjusted the oil furnace so the Hamptons would sleep comfortably on such an unseasonably cold night. Chi-Chi pulled her thin shawl tightly around her and slowly walked into the cold night. She began to hurry when she saw that the rain was steady and freezing on the old stepping stones that led to her cottage.

But the ice had made the stone path treacherous. Suddenly, her thin leather shoes slipped, and her legs flew out from under her. Her left elbow crashed into the rocks lining the pathway, sending sharp pains up her arm and out her shoulder.

Chi-Chi lay on the ground, her clothes soaked with freezing rain, unable to move.

About an hour later, Marion Hampton had finished reading in his study. He crossed the kitchen floor and heard a slight bump on the back porch. When he opened the door, he found Chi-Chi leaning on the doorframe, gasping for breath and holding her limp arm. She was wet and shivering. "Ellen!" he called and half-dragged Chi-Chi into a chair in the kitchen.

"Well, I'm no doctor, so I can't tell if it's broken or just banged a little." Marion tried to straighten Chi-Chi's arm.

"Mr. Marion, I don' knock 'em an' it be broke. I scared it get 'fect real soon."

He stepped back and scratched his head. "Maybe I need to send for Doc Hayes."

"On a night like this? It's too dangerous for him to

come out here in this weather," Mrs. Hampton admonished.

"Well, we can wrap it and get some hot tea in you and then see how it is in the morning," Mr. Hampton said.

"I surely hope it's better tomorrow. We have the party, the guests, and Edward coming. What are we going to do?" Ellen whined, wringing her hands and marching back and forth across the kitchen.

"Just fix her some tea and send her back to her cabin. We'll deal with her in the morning. Goodnight, all." Marion tightened his robe and left the room.

"They didn't even call a doctor?" Caleb asked, rubbing his elbow as he sat at the counter. Mattie's story had been so vivid that he felt every chill and every pain Chi-Chi had suffered that night.

"No, child, didn't do nothin' except wrap it and give her some tea. She spent a night of pain and cold in that drafty ol' cabin. She stay cold and wet all the way 'til day clean. All she did was lay in that bed and see her Bible by th' candlelight."

"Did she get help the next day?"

"The Hamptons was having their fancy party with all their friends, and Chi-Chi laid out in th' cabin burnin' up with fever, 'fected from head to toe. Mrs. Hampton was so mad that Chi-Chi couldn't work that mornin'. At the end, they sent someone to town to send a message 'cross the water to my daddy that she be real sick."

"Did he come and get her? Was she all right?"

"He come straight way when he got th' message. That was about two days later. They said that Chi-Chi be so weak that he had to carry her to th' back of th' gardener's truck, what drove them to th' ferry boat."

115

****

Mattie carried the basket of towels into the hall and set them at the foot of the stairs.

Caleb watched Mattie's every move. She returned to the kitchen and looked out the window. Sadness flooded her face as she continued her tale. "You see, Caleb, my daddy say that when he got to th' Hamptons' house, the miss'us be way too busy tellin' th' new girl about preparin' supper to even help them get Chi-Chi's things together. Daddy, he peek through th' big picture window and saw that purty table with th' lace cloth Chi-Chi be telling him 'bout in her letters. You know, she never got to as much as sit at that table or have a meal with those people. After all her hard work cookin' th' fine food an' polishin' th' silver."

Tears welled up in Mattie's eyes. "Anyways, in sight of a week, Chi-Chi be bury."

Mattie turned to the table and hurriedly set the dishes and silverware in their place. Caleb saw her pause to dab her eyes with her bright-colored apron.

"You be staying for supper, Caleb?" She crossed over to the glassware cabinet.

"Oh, I'm not sure. I'll have to call my mamma."

As Mattie folded the napkins, she shook her head and laughed.

"You know, young Caleb, things go 'round an' 'round in this world." Mattie pointed to the wood stacked in the corner for the parlor fireplace. "Look at that wood. It grow out in th' forest, then it be cut down. It be burnt and th' ashes thrown back to th' ground for another tree to take and grow. Then it be cut." Mattie took her arms and made a big circle like she was drawing on the teacher's chalkboard.

"All things be together in the Lord's time, you see?"

"Yes, Ma'am." Caleb wasn't sure why she was telling him this.

"Yessir, Caleb, Chi-Chi did get to be at that purty table with th' fine lace cloth after all."

"How did she do that? I thought you said she, uh, that she died." Caleb stopped stirring the beans, bewildered.

Mattie continued her tale.

****

The night was moonless as the dark figure prowled through the bushes in the Hamptons' backyard. Jonah Sullivan still felt a chill in the March night air and pulled his flimsy coat tighter to his skin, disclosing the bundle beneath. He knew it was planting time in the Hamptons' garden. The peas and onions were already in the ground to be followed by the warmer weather crops a month or so later.

"Dear Sista, 'dees folk will hav' yo spirit all da spring long." Jonah reached under his patchwork coat, held the delicate handmade urn with both hands and began a eulogy of sorts.

"Ma sista, Seer fo th' people, if'n you couldn't be a part of 'dis table in life, den yo spirit be a part of it in yo bury time. Their taint many t'ings what seem to bring yo da smile what you don had in dis house. I see, dear Chinue, God's own blessing, dat yo be a part o' these folk, fo'ever. Teach dem da ways, dear Chinue." He removed the fitted clay top and began to sprinkle the grave dirt, the dust of her spirit, between the rows of seedlings, chanting an ancient verse passed down through the island people. When the jar was empty, he returned it to the pouch under his coat and vanished through the night mist as quickly as he had come.

"You mean he…he…" Caleb wasn't sure he understood.

"Yessir, my daddy sprinkled Chi-Chi's bury dirt into their garden so her spirit be in th' plants they eat at that purty table."

"So…she was…kinda like…*fertilizer*?" Caleb was still trying to comprehend the meaning of the story.

"Yes, young Caleb, Chi-Chi's spirit rest in the buried dirt, she seasoned their table all th' spring long!" Mattie gave a hallelujah shout and clapped her hands. She crossed to the stove and sprinkled some salt into the beans.

"You sure you won't stay for supper, Caleb?"

Caleb stopped stirring and peered closer into the pot at the beans. "Uh, I-I'd better be getting home. My mama is expectin' me."

Without another word, he grabbed his coat and hurried out the back door.

Chapter 12

"Red sky at night still don't make no sense to me."
Albert's seat squeaked, and his fenders rattled on his old
Western Flyer bicycle. He leaned forward and forced the
pedals down, trying to keep up with Caleb gliding down
Cane Creek Road. "I mean, why would the sky be red at
night?"

"It's not night, but sunset. Anyways, that's what my
grandpa said this mornin'. The sky was red, so he thinks
some snow is on the way. You know, red sky at mornin',
sailors take warnin'. Red sky at night, sailors delight."

"Well, it sure is cold enough." Albert blew a stream
of fog from his chapped lips. The frigid air hit hard
against Caleb and Albert's faces as the two boys coasted
toward Marlee's house.

Christmas vacation had finally arrived, and they
were already into a routine. Caleb would rise early and
ride his bike to his grandparents' house, where he would
help his grandpa split and stack wood on the back porch.
Then, after a breakfast of scrambled eggs, grits, and his
grandma's buttermilk biscuits, he would ride to the
churchyard and meet Albert, and occasionally, Marlee.

"So why aren't we gonna play catch like yesterday?
I brought my stuff," Albert complained, glancing down
at the leather glove dangling from his bicycle seat.

"Marlee called last night and said she wanted us to
go ridin' with her this mornin'. We're supposed to meet

in front of her house."

"Oh, well, okay, let's go." Albert didn't have to be convinced when it came to Marlee. He lowered his head and stared at the road. Caleb cut his eyes at the boy riding beside him. What was going on? It was unlike Albert not to complain about going on a bike ride. He used his bicycle to get from one place to another, but pleasure riding wasn't his favorite thing to do. Caleb knew that Albert had a crush on Marlee, and since he was Caleb's friend, she usually just tolerated him. But since Albert was so nice to the kids at the Cedar Hill Children's Home, Marlee's feelings for him seemed to have softened into acceptance.

As the two boys rounded the curve on Cane Creek Road, Marlee came into sight, sitting on her bike at the end of the driveway. Ready for a morning ride, she was bundled in her Pendleton wool jacket, gloves, and scarf, her hair flowing from under a navy stocking cap.

"Hi, Marlee." Albert pulled his bike beside her and leaned on the handlebars. Aware that his nose was running, he wiped it with his mitten, caught himself, and hid the wet glove behind his back.

Marlee smiled and bent down to adjust the cuff of her blue jeans.

"So where're we goin'?" Caleb asked.

"I'm supposed to write a report for the Girl's Auxiliary at church."

"Yuck, homework from church?" Albert grimaced and shook his head.

"Well, sort of. It all goes in my GA booklet. Anyway, I thought I'd write about the poor people here in Fletcher."

"What, you mean like collect cans of food or

somethin'?" Caleb asked.

"No, mainly a report about how they live, stuff like that. So, I want to ride down into the hollow and see some of their houses up close."

"You mean the creek people? Ride our bikes down there?" Albert squeaked.

"Yeah. We won't be there long. I just want to look around, you know. Get some ideas about what to write."

Caleb studied Marlee's face for any signs that she was joking. He had always known that the creek divided their two worlds. The hollow was not the place for the three of them to explore. Maybe she was testing them, just like she did Halloween night.

"Why do you want to write about the Creek People? Isn't there other stuff you can write about?"

"I thought about it when we came to get the hams at Smoky's place, and I saw Annabelle and how she lived. I just wanna get a closer look at some of the houses and get some ideas for my report."

"I don't know. My mamma told me not to *ever* go 'cross the creek into the hollow." Albert shook his head slowly. "There are dogs down there, too. Big, mean ones." He held his hand up to his waist. "And I ain't goin' to Smoky's place, no siree bob!"

"I'm not going up to Smoky's house either. Anyway, you don't have to go. Caleb will go with me. Won't ya, Caleb?" Marlee pointed her bicycle out of her driveway and began to roll slowly into the street, adjusting her gloves.

Caleb followed. "Uh…sure. Wait up. Hey, Marlee, I have an idea. Maybe we could get one of our daddies to drive us there. Or Henry. Didn't he get his driver's license last month?" Caleb reasoned. "It'd be quicker and…well…you could see a lot more stuff."

"Oh, y'all are just a couple of old fraidy cats." Marlee stuffed her hair under her knit cap. "I'll go by myself, then." She took off down Cane Creek Road toward the bridge that divided the two worlds.

"And there's that old dirt road. It might tear up our bikes," Albert shouted. He reached down and gave his loose fender a shake.

"Marlee, hold up!" Caleb called. He peddled faster to catch her. She stopped on the side of the road when he pulled up beside her. They looked behind them to see Albert leaning on his handlebars in Marlee's driveway.

Caleb and Marlee rode together down Cane Creek Road toward the bridge when they heard Albert's rattling fender.

"Wait! Hold up! I'll go too, I guess." Albert was out of breath when he caught up with his friends. "Nothin' else to do. Might as well get dog bit, too."

"My protectors!" Marlee clasped her hands, held them under her chin, and batted her eyelashes. "Boy, do I feel safe!"

Caleb barked like a dog at Albert, and soon they were all laughing as they coasted down the hill toward the bridge that crossed Cane Creek.

The wooden planks were warped and cracked and could grab a bicycle tire, so the three had to walk their bikes across the bridge. The road on the other side of the bridge was unpaved and scarred with tire ruts that became mud holes on rainy days. They stopped and peered down the narrow road toward the hollow.

The bubbling of Cane Creek beneath them sounded like the murmur of distant voices, ominous words telling them this was far enough. To Caleb, it was as if the creek was offering a warning: "You don't belong here."

Gray clouds thickened, and the tall pines lining the road creaked and screamed as they swayed in the breeze, which seemed to get stronger every minute.

"I'm not sure I like this." Albert was still standing on the bridge with his bike leaning against his leg. He shifted his eyes from the swaying trees back to the road, which disappeared into the bleakness of the hollow.

Marlee didn't say a word. She hopped on her bike and cruised down the dirt road, maneuvering around the holes like an obstacle course. The three friends dodged tire ruts and jagged rocks as they continued their quest into the hollow where the creek people lived.

"Here comes a car!" Marlee shouted over her left shoulder as she pulled her bike into the pine straw lining the road. The old car crept by her so close that she could have touched the doors. Three young children peered out of the back window, noses pressed to the glass. None returned Marlee's wave.

"They were all dressed up like they were going to church or something," Marlee said after Caleb and Albert caught up with her. From behind them, an old truck bounced down the road and kicked up dust as it drove deeper into the hollow. They had to wave their hands to clear the red cloud from their faces. Albert spat and wiped his mouth on his sleeve.

"That man and woman were dressed up, too," Marlee said. She removed her sock cap and shook the dirt off the top.

"Maybe all the creek people dress up durin' the week, not just on Sunday," Albert said.

"Now, why would they go and do that?" Caleb pulled his bike onto the road. Marlee was already several yards in front.

"I don't know, and to tell you the truth, I don't care. Caleb, let's get out of here and go play catch, okay?" Albert pleaded.

But Caleb rode on toward Marlee. When he pulled beside her, she was leaning on her bike with one foot on the ground and one on the pedal. She appeared to be studying a house across the road from where they stood.

The small home sat back from the road, shaded by a large water oak tree with limbs that clutched the metal roof like long, gnarled fingers. The house was in dire need of repair, and a dozen or more cars and trucks were parked in the dusty yard. White flowers were attached to the mailbox post, and others were tacked to the door frame of the house. A few boys and girls played tag around the cars in the yard while the adults sat on the front porch steps, all dressed in Sunday clothes.

"What's goin' on?" Albert slowly rolled to a stop beside Caleb and Marlee.

"It looks like someone died," Caleb answered, pointing to the flowers hanging on the mailbox.

They turned and watched a family walk to the end of the driveway. The man had a sleeping baby cradled in his arms. The child wore a white gown with delicate lace stitching around the neck and sleeves and held tightly to the man's lapel. The mother's long hair, twisted into a bun, was piled high on her head and secured with navy-colored clips that matched her dress. Her high collar and long sleeves were trimmed with the same lace as on the baby's dress. A young boy in a dusty black suit strained against his mother's hand.

The boy stared at the bicycles as the family passed silently out of the drive and strolled down the road. The faces of the man and woman were drawn and solemn, their eyes fixed on the distant curve.

By then, more families had begun to leave the yard. Some drove old trucks or cars while others walked.

"I guess they're done with whatever they were doin'. Albert turned his bike around, eager to be on his way and finish this adventure of Marlee's.

"It must've been a wake, you know, where people sit up all night with the family and the dead person," Marlee said.

"You mean…uh…a dead person's in there?" Albert pointed to the house.

"Where'd you expect it to be, on the back porch?" Marlee rolled her eyes at Albert.

Several more cars pulled out from the end of the drive. All the families stared at the kids sitting on their bikes as the cars slowed. No one spoke or even waved.

At that moment, Caleb felt out of place. What was he doing here?

"Come on, let's get goin'," Caleb said. He turned his bike around and pedaled toward home. Marlee and Albert followed behind.

"When my grandpa died, he was at a funeral home. Havin' them at your house, boy, that would be kinda eerie. I guess the weird creek people don't mind that sort of thing," Albert said when he caught up with Caleb.

Marlee stopped her bike and skidded her feet on the road. "So, I guess I'm weird too! My grandpa was at my grandma's house, and we stayed there all night." Marlee bit her bottom lip and rapidly pedaled up the dirt road, leaving Caleb and Albert.

Caleb slapped Albert lightly on his arm. "Just don't say nothin' about her grandpa, okay?"

"What'd I say? I didn't know anythin' about that," Albert whined. "I mean, my mama sent a casserole and all, but I never went to her grandma's house. How was I supposed to know?"

Caleb rode on. Memories of last summer when Marlee's grandfather died, filtered into his mind.

It was about the last week in July, and they were catching crawdads in Cane Creek when Henry suddenly appeared on the creek bank. Caleb immediately noticed his red eyes and grim expression.

"Marlee, you better get on home. We're goin' over to Grandma's. Grandpa Patterson died a little while ago."

Marlee stood still in the creek, holding the rock she had turned over while searching for a crawdad. Without a word, she dropped her bucket into the water, grabbed her shoes lying by the creek, and ran down the trail. The crawdads scurried out of the bucket to freedom as Marlee disappeared through the foliage. Henry followed slowly behind.

Caleb emptied his bucket, then picked up Marlee's. She wouldn't mind if the crawdads got away; after all, nature sometimes has a way of changing priorities. A few minutes earlier, he and Marlee had been laughing and collecting critters, and now he was alone with just the sounds of the creek. He stood there for a few minutes. The water swirled gently around his ankles, making tiny whirlpools and gurgling voices. He knew it was time to go home.

Caleb had never been to a wake before. He had made a couple of funeral home visits for church members and once for a great uncle, but he had never experienced the loss of someone close to him.

He vividly remembered the fireflies in the front yard

of Marlee's grandmother's house. They made him think of Christmas lights, although it was a humid July night. He spent most of the evening on the long porch, leaning against the banister, watching the fireflies, and wishing he had a mayonnaise jar and his old clothes. He couldn't remember ever wearing his Sunday outfit this late at night.

Caleb's mother made him come inside and fix a plate of food brought by the ladies from the church, but he took it back out to the porch and ate. It was too sad in there. He didn't think he could look inside Marlee's grandmother's house again without picturing the open casket in the parlor surrounded by what looked like a garden of flowers on metal stands.

It was almost midnight, and Caleb was alone on the porch except for Marlee's two younger cousins, asleep in the wooden swing when Marlee came out and sat beside Caleb on the steps. They didn't say much, and her grandfather was never mentioned. Caleb saw Marlee's red eyes and knew she had been crying, but they just sat, watched the fireflies, and listened to the katydids as their drone increased and then waned into periodic silence. Occasionally, the screen door banged shut, and one of the men strolled onto the porch for a smoke. The boys in the swing stirred but never woke.

As Caleb pedaled his bike up the dirt road, he remembered those drawn, concerned expressions on the adults' faces at Grandpa Patterson's wake. They were the same tense faces and vacant eyes the man and woman had worn today as they had left the yard.

When the boys rounded the curve, they saw Marlee's bicycle lying in the dirt, the back tire still spinning. Marlee sat in the pine straw and held her leg.

One knee of her jeans was torn. When she saw Caleb and Albert coming, she quickly wiped her eyes with her sleeve. She pushed her hand against the red dirt road and tried to stand. Favoring one leg, she finally stood and limped toward her bicycle.

"What happened?" Caleb jumped from his bike and ran over to Marlee.

"I hit one of these dang tire ruts and fell."

"You okay?" Albert asked. "Sorry if I made you mad or somethin'. All I meant was—

"You didn't make me fall," Marlee interrupted. "I just hit one of these—doggone it!" She screamed and kicked her bike with her good leg. "Now the tire is busted!"

Caleb lifted Marlee's bike out of the dirt.

"Yep, she's flat all right. Looks like we push 'em home."

"Y'all go on. I'll catch up with you later," Marlee said as she balanced the bike and started to push it up the dirt road, limping with every step.

Just then, a pickup truck roared around the curve, barely missing Caleb's bike lying crossways in the lane. The old truck slid to a stop, and a man got out and angrily slammed the door. "You kids tryin' ta git kilt?"

At first, Caleb and Marlee didn't recognize Smoky Pruitt in his black Sunday suit. Even dressed up, he looked out of place. His coat was tight and too short for his long-sleeved white shirt poking out beneath the cuff. A thin black tie hung loose and crooked around his open shirt collar.

"Uh…uh…I had a wreck and a flat tire and…well…" Marlee, stumbling with her words, spread her arms helplessly. Smoky bent down and squeezed her front tire between his long index finger and thumb.

Caleb stood to the side of the road but he could smell a combination of wood smoke and alcohol on Smoky's wool suit. Caleb had only smelled whisky a couple of times in his life.

"This ain't no bike-ridin' road," Smoky barked.

"Yessir," Marlee said.

"Yessir," Caleb added. Albert remained beside his bike at the woods' edge, not moving a muscle, but his eyes widened as he watched every move Smoky Pruitt made.

"Looks like ya banged yer leg up there." Smoky pointed at Marlee's torn blue jeans, slightly stained with blood.

"Oh, yes, sir, but it's just a scratch."

"Even scratches git 'fected," he snapped. "Y'all climb on up in the back of th' truck." Smoky picked up Marlee's bicycle, laid it in the truck bed, and placed Caleb's bike there too.

Then Smoky looked at Albert. "Hey, boy, ya ridin' wif 'em?"

"Uh…well…my bike's okay, but…"

"C'mon Albert, get in," Caleb said, already standing in the truck bed. Albert reluctantly rolled his bike to the tailgate.

The truck bounded up the dirt road, and the kids had to hold the pile of bikes in place with their feet while they leaned against the cab. At first, no one spoke. After a few minutes, Marlee whispered, "Wonder how far he's gonna take us?"

"Boy, I'm just glad we're not goin' down to his house," Albert said. "Don't want to wind up in one of them smokehouses."

"Shush-up! He might hear you!" Marlee said through her clenched teeth.

Caleb sat up straight and peered over the pile of bikes. "I think he's going to your house, Marlee."

"How does he know where I live?"

"You reckon he knows where we all live?" Albert asked.

The old truck turned into the bottom of Marlee's driveway and jerked to a stop. The kids sat still when they heard the loud creak of the truck door opening.

"Y'all c'n jump down now," Smoky ordered, reaching for the bicycles. When he finished unloading, he climbed back into the truck without a word.

"Uh, thank you, Mr. Pruitt." Marlee stood beside the gravel driveway. Smoky gave a slight nod and then began to close the door. Before it shut, Marlee added, "Tell Annabelle I said…Merry Christmas!"

He paused and opened his mouth but then closed it tightly. He shut the door, forced the gearshift into reverse, and backed into the road.

"Praise the Lord, we're alive!" Albert shouted as he picked up his bike. "I just knew we were goin' to wind up as next year's hams."

"Oh, you and Henry! He oughta be your brother instead of mine." Marlee started pushing her bike up the drive, limping slightly.

"Need any help?" Caleb reached for her bike as he walked up the gravel drive.

"No, y'all go on. I'm gonna clean up my knee and work on my project."

"Okay. Meet up at the church tomorrow?"

"I'm going shopping with Mama tomorrow, but I'll see you Christmas Eve as usual." She left Caleb and hobbled on toward her house.

Caleb and Albert rode toward the church. Compared to the rough road of the hollow, the asphalt felt good under their tires, but the air seemed colder now that the tall pines didn't protect them.

"You gettin' with Marlee on Christmas Eve?" Albert asked.

"Yeah. Our families always get together for salmon stew on Christmas Eve. We've done it as far back as I can remember."

"Did you get Marlee a present?"

"Yeah. I got her a black stuffed bear from Cherokee last summer. She loves that sorta thing."

"Wonder if I oughta get her somethin'?"

"Naw, I doubt she's got you anythin'," Caleb spoke before he thought, and he didn't intend to sound harsh. "I mean, y'all don't usually do presents, but you could come over later and eat some of my mama's fruitcake if you wanna."

"That'd be fun. 'Bout all we do on Christmas Eve is sit around watching Christmas shows on TV and try to calm Alice down. She gets so crazy!"

The boys rolled into the churchyard and stopped in front of the Nativity scene. The wooden figures shook from the wintry breeze.

The cut-plywood wise men and shepherds stood about six feet tall around the empty manger where Mary and Joseph kneeled. Behind them lay the cow, donkey, and sheep, cut-outs in the makeshift stable. The live animals weren't coming until right before Christmas Eve.

The two friends slid off their bicycles and meandered through the nativity scene. Caleb stopped and placed his arm around one of the wise men like they were good buddies. "This wise man is my favorite."

But Albert wasn't listening. He stood by a shepherd boy in front of the empty manger. "Is Marlee gonna bring another doll out here for the baby Jesus?"

"Don't know. Guess so."

"Wonder who took it?"

Caleb shrugged. Marlee thinks some kid who don't know much about Christmas or just wants a doll took it. I think it's Bobby Henderson playing a prank."

"Yeah, sounds like something he'd do. Hey, look." Albert spread his arms and hands wide and began turning in circles. "It's snowing!"

The two boys looked into the gray sky and watched the flakes swirl in the cold afternoon breeze. They yelped and ran around the churchyard, trying to catch snowflakes on the tips of their tongue.

Chapter 13

Caleb could feel the change. A couple of years ago, the first thing he and Marlee would do on Christmas Eve was tear open the presents they gave each other and start playing on the living room floor. But tonight, he was more excited about what he was giving Marlee than the present he was getting. The Pattersons arrived just as he finished wrapping Marlee's present. Caleb's mother opened the door and chimed a cheerful "Merry Christmas!" Marlee was carrying what appeared to be a pie wrapped in foil while Henry held tight to a jug of apple cider. Mr. Patterson remained on the porch and finished his cigarette, joined by Caleb's dad.

"Y'all can take that to the kitchen," Caleb's mother instructed. After setting the cider on the kitchen table, Henry retreated to the den and turned on the TV.

Caleb and Marlee went to the living room and sat under the Christmas tree.

"What is that?" Marlee pointed to the colorful package tucked under Caleb's arm. He

playfully searched the floor behind him. "I don't know what you're talkin' about."

Marlee pulled a small gift from her sweater pocket. "Okay, well, I guess I'll have to find someone else to give this to."

"On the count of three, let's trade," Caleb offered. "One…two…"

Marlee grabbed the present from Caleb and didn't waste any time ripping open the package. "Oh, I *love* it!" Marlee snuggled the black bear to her chest and hugged it tightly.

"I got it in Cherokee last summer. I know you like bears, and this one looks like the real thing."

"I'll keep him next to my pillow every night." Marlee held the bear up to her face, touching her nose to the black plastic nose of the bear. "I've got to think up a name."

"How about Smoky?"

Marlee glared at Caleb as if she were peering over a pair of reading glasses.

"You know, like…Smoky the Bear?"

"I don't think so, but I'm sure I'll think of something. Anyway, go ahead and open yours." Marlee handed him the present with one hand and clutched the bear with the other.

Caleb took the small package and shook it next to his ear. "Sounds like bullets!" he teased.

"Go on, open it," Marlee urged impatiently.

"Wow, this is neat!" Caleb held up the shiny I.D. bracelet so that it glimmered with a rainbow of colors from the lights on the Christmas tree. He took his fingers and traced over the engraved letters on the bracelet. *Caleb* was written in a beautiful cursive script. He clipped the bracelet on his wrist and lifted it proudly for Marlee to see. It slid down his thin arm from hand to elbow.

"You can take out a few links if you want to."

"I love it! I'll wear it every day. Thank you!"

"I picked it out myself. Mama said I shouldn't get jewelry for a boy, but I told her how everyone at school had them."

"Come on, folks, stew's on!" Mrs. Austin announced, sticking her head around the corner from the kitchen. They could hear the rattle of the Christmas china being taken from the hutch in the dining room and set on the large table. The house was filled with the strong smell of the salmon stew simmering in its milk broth, mingling with the spicy aroma of hot apple cider.

Immediately, the TV in the den clicked off, and the footsteps of Caleb's dad, Mr. Patterson, and Henry clamored across the hardwood floors. Caleb and Henry always exchanged comic books at Christmas. They didn't call it a present since they were not wrapped. Caleb gave Henry a *Fantastic Four,* and Caleb got a *Flash.*

The adults took their place in the dining room while Caleb, Marlee, and Henry sat at a card table Caleb's dad had set up in the den.

"Why do you do that?" Marlee shrieked, watching Henry hold the ketchup bottle over his stew. "It's yucky!"

Henry shook an extra-large blob of ketchup into his bowl. Stew splattered onto the table, and Henry and Caleb laughed.

"Mama, Henry's making a mess!"

"You shush up!" Henry leaned his chair to the side to see into the dining room. But he leaned too far and lost his balance. The ladderback chair crashed to the hardwood and was followed by the ceaseless clang of his spoon as it somersaulted and came to rest under the TV set.

Caleb spewed his first sip of stew over the table. "What's goin' on in there?" Mrs. Patterson's voice came from the dining room.

"Nothing, Mama." Marlee laughed . "Henry's just being his clumsy ol' self, as usual!"

"Look at this mess!" Mrs. Patterson stood in the doorway with her hands on her hips. "Henry, go get a dishcloth and clean this up. And get your spoon out from under the TV."

"But Mama, it was Marlee. She—"

"Just do what I say and sit back down and behave. Set an example for the younger ones." At that, she turned and left the room.

Henry slouched his way to the kitchen to get the dishcloth and tossed it onto the card table in front of Marlee. "You always get me in trouble."

"Me? What'd I do? You're the one who fell all over the room," Marlee flailed her arms in the air, imitating Henry.

Henry stuck out his tongue and continued eating his soup in loud slurps, knowing how it would irritate Marlee.

"Oh, Caleb, we stopped by and checked on Daisy and Gertrude at the manger on our way here. I hope they don't get too cold tonight," Marlee said.

"I don't think they will," Caleb replied.

"They're farm animals. They're used to the cold," Henry demanded.

"Yeah, Henry's right. And they have the stable with hay and everythin'."

"I know, it's just…well, it's Christmas."

"So? Are you afraid Santa might not find 'em?" Henry chuckled at his joke and poked Caleb in the ribs. "After all, they're supposed to be in the barn on Christmas Eve." Henry gulped another spoonful of stew and glanced up at Marlee. " 'Specially at midnight."

Caleb and Marlee exchanged puzzled expressions.

"Why're they supposed to be there at midnight?" Marlee asked.

Henry made a loud slurp of his stew and ignored Marlee.

"Henry!" Marlee banged her spoon on the table. "Why midnight?"

"Don't you know nothin'? All farm animals bow to pray at midnight on Christmas Eve, actually, Christmas morning. Ever'one knows that!"

"Oh, pooh on you."

Caleb leaned toward Marlee. "You know, seems like I've heard that too."

Marlee glared at Caleb. "So now you're on Henry's side!"

"No, I mean, I really have heard that somewhere, you know, about the animals prayin'. Maybe it was my Grandpa or Mattie, but I've heard that about farm animals."

Henry picked up his empty bowl and walked toward the kitchen. "Think I'll have some more stew and read my comic book."

"Wait! Where'd you hear that about the animals at midnight?" Marlee asked.

"Don't know. I guess, like Caleb did, from somebody. I mean, don't you believe the Dogwood blossom shows Jesus' hands?"

"Well, yeah, but I've seen that. And they talk about it in church every Easter. But I haven't heard them talk about this."

"Believe what you want. Only one way to find out, though." Henry winked at Caleb before disappearing into the kitchen.

While Caleb crunched a handful of crackers into his stew, Marlee sat, staring absently out the window across the den. He watched her take a clump of hair and twist it around her finger into a tight curl. Caleb knew Marlee was hatching some sort of plan. And he was right.

"Wouldn't that be neat? I mean, what if they did bow their heads?"

"Yeah, but remember Henry and his wild stories? You're the one always warning me 'bout listening to him." Caleb nodded toward the kitchen.

"I know, but think about it: why couldn't they bow? After all, God made them, too. They were there when Jesus was born. It makes perfect sense."

Caleb didn't respond. Instead, he chased a large piece of salmon around his bowl while halfway listening to Henry talking to the men in the next room about deer season.

"Why don't we go see them tonight?" Marlee whispered, leaning toward Caleb.

"Tonight? You mean go to the church…at midnight?"

"Well, that's when they bow, so, of course, at midnight."

"I don't know if our folks—"

"Oh, they'll stay here late like they did last Christmas. Remember how we fell asleep under the tree while they drank coffee and ate cheesecake 'til almost two o'clock?"

"Yeah, I must have been lookin' at the lights because I had a dream that I was layin' on a big cloud of cotton candy." Caleb laughed.

"We can tell them we're gonna lay out in the

backyard and look for the Christmas star. You know they'll believe that. Then we can sneak down to the church. We'll be back before anyone knows we're gone."

"I don't know. What if—"

Marlee slid from her chair and walked back and forth in front of the table like a caged animal. Her finger twisted her hair into a tight curl as she devised their plan. "We can start off looking at the stars, so it won't be a lie. Then, just before midnight, we'll cut across the field to Cane Creek Road and up to the church. That's the shortest way."

"But…what if…I mean—" Caleb then fell silent. He knew what he would be doing at midnight.

Chapter 14

Cane Creek Road was darker than Caleb had imagined. As he and Marlee topped the hill near the church, the street lamp cast a dim glow across the parking lot, tossing a meager hint of light toward the red brick building. The church stood dark and lonely. No light poured through the stained-glass windows to form colored arches on the ground below. On this Christmas Eve night, the bleak building stood in silent expectation, waiting to be filled with activity once again.

In sharp contrast to the dark, cold church, the stable on the front lawn glowed warmly from the floodlights Caleb and the men had placed around the scene. Inside the stable, a cone of light shone across a plywood angel who stood with arms outstretched between Mary and Joseph. Daisy and Gertrude snuggled against several bales of straw in the back of the stable, asleep. The outside light cast oversized shadows of wise men across the bare limbs of the hickory trees beyond.

"Let's go over there behind those bushes." Marlee pointed to a boxwood hedge between the church and the nativity scene. A thin layer of snow crunched under their knees as they knelt behind the shrub to watch the animals.

"How much longer till midnight?" Marlee peered over, trying to see Caleb's watch. Caleb held his arm up to catch the light on his watch. The ID bracelet shimmered and slid under the sleeve of his winter coat.

"It's five till."

The two huddled, careful not to make a sound. The cold, dampness seeped through the knees of their jeans. Fog coming from their mouths dissipated like the smoke from the neighboring houses.

Quietly, they waited and watched.

The animals began to stir. Gertrude jumped to her feet, eyes wide, followed by Daisy. Marlee's breath quickened, and she grabbed Caleb's wrist and pulled him close to her. They stared in expectation as the animals moved about nervously. An ancient chord had been struck.

"Are they 'bout to…kneel?" Marlee could hardly say the words. She grabbed Caleb's arm and pulled him close to her.

"They sense somethin'." Caleb turned his head and scanned the woods beyond.

A stick popped in the underbrush across from where Caleb and Marlee knelt. They heard feet rustling the dead leaves on the forest floor.

"Somethin's comin'," whispered Caleb. He could hear the thump of his own heartbeat, and he wondered if Marlee could hear it, too.

Marlee tightened her grip on Caleb's wrist. "Albert? You said you invited him to come over for pie. Would he be coming through the woods?" she whispered.

Caleb shook his head as he shifted his eyes around the area. "He's afraid of the woods at night; besides, he doesn't know we are here. We didn't even tell our folks, and anyway, he wouldn't come this late.

Two dark figures emerged from the shadows.

"Look at—" Marlee gasped and leaned forward,

almost sticking her head through the boxwood. The dim streetlight cast a pale glimmer onto Annabelle Pruitt's face. She held the hand of a younger girl who clutched a bundle close to her body with her right arm. The two girls crunched through the snow toward the stable.

"It's Annabelle and...somebody with her! Her sister?" Marlee, barely able to contain her excitement, was half-risen from her crouching position.

Caleb didn't respond except to grab Marlee's arm and pull her back beside him. "Shh!" He glanced around nervously for any signs of Smoky Pruitt and his hound dogs. Caleb's thoughts were racing. Why would Annabelle and this little girl be alone, walking through the woods at midnight? What if Smoky's with them, or, even worse, what if they're not supposed to be here, and he catches them? What if he sees us? Smoky might think Marlee and I had something to do with it. Caleb's breath quickened.

Marlee leaned over to get her balance and began to stand. "Let's go see what they're doin'."

"No!" Caleb said with a loud whisper. He yanked Marlee's arm. "Let's just watch from here. See what they're up to. You don't want to scare them away."

Annabelle was dressed the same as the last time they had seen her at Harper's Store. She kept her coat closed around her tiny body with her free hand.

Annabelle reached for the bundle that the other girl held tightly. "C'mon now, Abigail, it's time. It's Christmas mornin' by now."

Caleb glanced at his watch. She was right. It was Christmas morning.

Abigail looked up at her sister through a tangle of brown hair, which traced across the black smudges on her face. She opened the burlap bundle and handed a doll to Annabelle.

"My doll! They had my doll!" Marlee exclaimed.

Without thinking, Caleb reached over to put his hand across Marlee's mouth, but instead, he caught himself, put his fingers to his lips, and glared at her.

Annabelle took the doll to the manger and gently laid it on the hay.

"Ain't no baby till Christmas Day. That's when th' baby Jesus was bornt. 'Member th' story I tolt ta ya? The one mamma tolt ta me?" Annabelle took her younger sister by the hand, and they both knelt by of the manger. Abigail reached over and gently brushed a strand of hay from the doll's face. "They wrapped th' baby in swatling clothes an' lyed 'im in th' manger 'cause they weren't no room a' tall in th' house," Annabelle continued. "Mama used ta read it all ta me from her Bible. I c'n read some of th' words now, but I 'member most of it anyhow. Mama said he was bornt special. Kinda like me."

Abigail continued to pat the head of the doll. "Baby." She listened intently to her sister, sometimes forming the words with her own lips.

Annabelle stood and circled the manger and told the story to her sister. Abigail's eyes widened as she watched her big sister's expressions and followed her gestures.

"Mama used ta say Jesus was th' light of th' world, like th' can'le burnin' bright on her table. Jus' like th' one burnin' in th' smokehouse. Ya don't cover up a can'le. Ya let it be bright for ever'one ta see." Annabelle spread her arms out wide to emphasize her statement. "Mama'd say it's not the thangs what a person has that's 'portant. It's what's in here." She reached and touched her sister's chest. Abigail looked at where her sister pointed and placed her hand over her heart.

Caleb and Marlee still knelt on the cold ground. Annabelle's words floated through the shadowy churchyard, and the warm glow from the stable encircled the two girls in front of the manger. The words of this little creek girl from the hollow, cloaked with a thick rural accent, described the story of the first Christmas more simply and sincerely than Caleb had ever heard.

Chapter 15

It was Christmas Day. For Caleb, this day had always been a celebration of the senses. The smell of the cedar Christmas tree and the rustle of gift wrap paper, coupled with smiling faces and warm hugs from his family, heightened the excitement of Christmas morning.

The pungent aroma of cornbread dressing drifted from grandma's oven and sought out every nose in the house. By noon, most of the extended Austin family had arrived, and the annual Christmas get-together was well underway, complete with Aunt Lil playing *Jingle Bells* on his grandparents' old upright piano. Apron-clad mothers bustled around the kitchen, and the older men held council on the front porch, smoking their cigarettes and pipes. Caleb used this opportunity to show off the new 20-gauge shotgun he had gotten for Christmas.

After the large meal, Caleb, his dad, and his grandpa spent the rest of the afternoon shooting cans and bottles in the back of his grandparents' property, but unlike Thanksgiving, Caleb now had his own gun to use. He inhaled the smell of the gunpowder that hung in the air. He loved this. It was warm for Christmas Day, and the snow from the night before had already melted except for a few frosty patches under shrubbery. Caleb had to squint from the sun when the old drink cans were tossed into the air. Soon, the thunderous boom would be heard, and the rumpled can would rocket across the field and rest beneath the pines.

****

The stir of Christmas activities had crowded the events of Christmas Eve from Caleb's mind. For the last two days, his focus had been on food, relatives, and gifts, but now life was beginning to feel more regular.

The day after Christmas, Caleb helped his dad and grandpa repair the old outbuilding on the back of their lot, where they stored lawnmowers, a tiller, and a wide assortment of garden tools. This year, Caleb's grandpa gave him his first real toolbox and tools for Christmas. Caleb remembered when he had opened the gray metal box. The shiny surfaces of the tools were not yet blemished or worn. He recalled the sheer power he had felt when he had held the claw hammer and smacked it against the palm of his hand.

Now, he worked alongside the other two men using his new tools. The muscles in his forearm strained as he swung the hammer and heard it crack against the nail head. The knocking rhythm echoed off the mountainside. Caleb's hammer matched the cadence of the others, and when the plywood roof was in place, his father slapped him on the back of his sweat-soaked shirt. "Good job," he said, and Caleb swelled with pride. Those two words rang in his ears all afternoon.

Caleb sawed boards and hammered roofing tiles most of that afternoon, and every little while, he took a break. The three men leaned against the repaired outbuilding and drank iced water from mason jars.

That evening, after supper, Caleb's parents and grandparents sat at the dining table sipping cups of coffee. Caleb sat alone on the living room couch, leafing through his new comic book when, out of the corner of his eye, he spotted the nativity scene on the mantle. His grandpa had hand-carved these figures many years before Caleb was born.

He set his book aside and walked to the fireplace. Every year before Christmas, when his dad removed the wooden figures from their linen wrappings, he rubbed linseed oil into the dark walnut wood. Caleb took the statue of Joseph and ran his fingers delicately along the smooth lines, admiring his grandpa's craftsmanship.

Then Caleb picked up one of the wise men and turned it over in his hand, guiding his fingers over the well-oiled wood. Holding the figure, he thought of what he and Marlee had witnessed Christmas Eve at the church's Nativity scene. Annabelle's words returned to him: "It's not the thangs what a person has that's 'portant. It's what's in here."

Caleb dropped back on the couch and propped his head on a cushion. With only the muffled voices of the adults in the dining room and his fingers still rubbing the wooden figure, Caleb dozed off to sleep.

Chapter 16

The next day, Caleb met Marlee at her driveway, and they strolled up Cane Creek Road toward the church.

"So, did you tell your Mama about Christmas Eve? I mean, about us sneaking out and seeing the girls?" Marlee asked.

"Yeah. She wasn't too mad about it. 'Course, she kinda had to act like she was, but I could tell she wasn't."

"My mama didn't like it much, but then she said maybe it was the Lord's way for us to find out about Abigail. What did your mama say about the girls? Can she find out anything from the people she knows?"

"She said she'd call the social services and see what they had to say. She's not sure if anything can be done unless some law's been broken."

"Well, since no one knew about her, surely that's against the law. I mean, you can't just keep people like that, especially in a smokehouse."

"We don't know if they live in the smokehouse. Not for certain, anyways. They might just stay out there some and play. Kinda like when I go camping. Anyway, do you want to head down to Turtle Rock?" Caleb asked. "It's been a while since we've been there."

Marlee hesitated. "I wanted to go by the church and get my doll. They'll be taking the nativity scene down soon, but we can go by there after we go to the creek."

The two friends headed down Cane Creek Road and

then took the path to Cane Creek. They were in no hurry since it was still Christmas break, and the holiday rush was over. They talked about Christmas and everything that had happened the last few days as they ambled along the creek bank. The two friends quietly tossed acorns into the water and watched them float lazily around rocks and swirl in tiny whirlpools near the creek bank.

Suddenly, there was a stir in the brush on the opposite side. Annabelle Pruitt stood up, her eyes wide from being startled.

Caleb heard Marlee gasp with alarm. No one moved for several seconds, and then Annabelle bent over and stirred the ground with a stick. She stood, holding what appeared to be a handful of dried weeds, turned, and instantly disappeared into the brush. Marlee ran to the edge of the creek.

"Annabelle! You there? We want to talk to you! Where'd you go?"

Caleb peered through the woods for any sign of Smoky or his dogs. "I think we oughta get out of here."

Marlee didn't listen. She immediately studied the creek bank for a place to cross over to the other side. A few feet away, she saw a line of boulders jutting out of the stream. Without a word, Marlee skillfully skipped across the rocks and pulled herself onto the bank, avoiding the cold creek water.

Protesting, Caleb followed, not knowing what they were going to do next. "Marlee! I don't think this is such a good idea." Caleb's plea was ignored.

Marlee fought through the vines and brambles until she was where Annabelle had stood.

Caleb caught up to her a moment later.

"What are we doing here? Smoky could be

anywhere." Caleb was breathing heavily from fear and running after Marlee.

"I thought she might still be over here. I want to know what she was doing and ask her about—"

"Marlee, why is that so important?" Caleb interrupted. His voice was cloaked with irritation.

"Because I want to find out about…hey, look!" Marlee bent over and began raking leaves aside with her fingers. "Something is buried here!"

Caleb carefully leaned in beside Marlee, both studying the ground where Annabelle had been standing. "Maybe it's just where some critter dug a hole, that's all."

"Yeah, some critter named Annabelle!" Marlee was scooping handfuls of loose dirt from the hole when her fingers hit what sounded like a piece of metal. "There's something here, Caleb. Help me dig."

The two friends knelt on the forest floor and pushed aside the cold soil and dead leaves. After a couple of minutes of digging, a rusted metal handle appeared.

"It's a box! That's what Annabelle was trying to cover up when we saw her!" Marlee was so excited that her hands were shaking. "Let's pull it out of here and see what's in it."

Caleb was cautious but just as curious as Malee. He pictured a cache of money or maybe the lost Confederate gold he'd heard from his grandpa's tales, but he kept his thoughts to himself.

Together, they hoisted the box out from the ground and set it beside the hole. The case was about the size of a shoe box but with a top handle and hinges in the back. There was a clasp in front, but no lock. Caleb straightened and scanned the woods for signs of

Annabelle or Smoky. The only sound he could hear was the murmur of the water flowing over the rocks. He was not comfortable on this side of the creek. Caleb jumped when he heard the scream of rusted hinges. Marlee had opened the box.

An embroidered handkerchief covered the contents. Marlee carefully pulled the delicate cloth aside. Underneath was a tattered Bible. Marlee lifted the Bible from the box.

"This must be Annabelle's mother's Bible. Remember Christmas Eve? She told Abigail that her mother read to her." A cloth bookmark was inserted between the thin pages. Marlee opened the Bible to the marked passages. "Luke 20! The Christmas story! I bet she read this to Abigail on Christmas!"

Is there anything else in the box?" Caleb asked.

Marlee closed the Bible and laid it in her lap. "Just these dried plants. I wonder what it is? Does it mean something?" Marlee held the plant to her nose. "It smells familiar. And it looks like the same stuff Anabelle had in her hands a few minutes ago. I wonder why she wanted these plants?" Marlee handed the small bouquet to Caleb, who inspected the dried leaves and roots.

"I have no idea, but I bet she was puttin' them in here when she saw us," Caleb reasoned.

"Or, maybe she was taking some out." Marlee began twisting her curls as she talked.

Caleb stood and studied the forest, looking deep through the trees. "I don't know, but we better put this back and get outta here."

Marlee replaced the Bible and handkerchief and carefully lowered the box into the shallow hole. Caleb scooped dirt over the box lid and scattered dried leaves across the disturbed area.

"What are you doing with those?" Caleb pointed to the handful of dried plants Marlee had taken from the box.

"I want to find out what they are. Why did Annabelle have them?"

"Well, too late to put them back now. Let's go!" Caleb pulled Marlee's arm, and the two hurried across the creek and back down the trail.

****

Deep in thought, the two friends walked along the gravel drive that led to the church. Caleb broke the silence.

"Hey, Marlee. I think maybe we shouldn't tell anyone about the box we found. I mean, we don't want someone else going lookin' for it."

Marlee nodded in agreement. "Our secret." She held up her pinky finger, and Caleb wrapped his finger around hers and shook.

Once in the churchyard, they stopped in front of the Nativity scene. The animals had been picked up the day after Christmas, but the plywood figures were still standing beside the manger, which held Marlee's swaddled doll.

Marlee stuck the plants in her jacket pocket. She bent down, picked up the doll and held it to her nose. "Still smells like wood smoke. But you know something? Next year, I think I'll wait till Christmas morning to put the doll out here."

"I've got joy like a fountain, I've got joy like a fountain, I've got joy like a fountain in my soul..."

Caleb and Marlee turned to see Mattie moseying up the road, singing; her face turned toward the sky. When

152

she saw the children, she held her hand up in greeting and turned into the churchyard.

"How're two of my fav-o-rite young'uns this mornin'?"

"Just fine," Marlee said.

"Are you going to my grandparents'?" Caleb asked.

"Yessir. James—he's my oldest son—just let me out back there at th' railroad tracks. Said he's some shoppin' to do." She sat down on a bale of straw in front of the Nativity scene. "Catch my breath, and I'll be on my way. So, is that th' baby Jesus you holdin' there?"

"Yes, ma'am."

"Thought I heard that someone took the doll again this year."

"Yes, ma'am, they did. But they brought it back on Christmas Eve. Well, actually, it was Christmas morning," Marlee said.

"Land sakes alive, child. Who be doin' somethin' like that?"

Caleb and Marlee looked at each other. Caleb broke the silence. "Uh, we were here when they brought it back."

"It was midnight on Christmas Eve," Marlee added.

"What in this ol' world was you two doin' out here at midnight? And on Christmas Eve! You should've been home tucked in your beds." Mattie leaned close toward Caleb.

"Well," Caleb explained, "Henry told us that all the farm animals bowed their heads at midnight on Christmas Eve. Not that we believed him, of course, but we just wanted to come see for ourselves."

"My daddy told me th' same tale back on th' island when I be just a wee thing." Mattie held her hand out to

153

show her height. "But I never did get to go and see it. So, what happened? Did the animals bow, like my daddy said?"

"Your daddy told you about it?" Caleb stared in disbelief. He pulled up a bale of straw close to where Mattie was sitting. Marlee sat beside him, and he and Marlee told Mattie the story of their adventure on Christmas Eve.

When they finished the story, Mattie threw her hands over her head and slapped them onto her knees. "Oh my! Glory be to th' Lord! Outta th' mouth of babes! I knew she was a special child. I knew it from th' time she was born."

"But what about Abigail? Were you there when she was born, too?" Marlee asked.

"No, I done quit midwifing when that next child was borned. Some folks say her mama birthed that baby all alone and come down with th' consumption sometime after. That's what killed her, you know. I come by with some root tea but ol' Smoky he opened th' door, took it, closed it in my face before I could even get a look." Mattie gazed off into the distance, rocking and coddling the doll as if it were a real baby.

"We told my mama about seeing Abigail. She's going to call the welfare people," Caleb said.

"We think she must live in one of those smokehouses down at Smoky Pruitts' place," Marlee added.

"My, my, what a special child that Annabelle be. I knew when I saw th' veil at her birthin' she sees things in ways nobody else's could. Her mama knew it too, that's why she read to her so much outta th' Good Book."

"But is that why she quit goin' to school? To take

154

care of Abigail, you think?" Marlee asked.

Mattie tightened her lips into a thousand tiny wrinkles. "Well, child, could be, but I 'spose folks just be afraid of somethin' they don't know 'bout. Many folks in these mountains here just can't take to someone like Annabelle. Of course, there's a lot of special chil'en that ain't been understood." Mattie gave a slight chuckle and stroked the doll's head. "So, what you be doin' with the ginger root?" Mattie pointed to the dried plants sticking out of Marlee's jacket pocket.

Marlee glanced at Caleb, remembering their pinky swear.

"Um…we were just down at Turtle Rock, and they were lying on the ground." Marlee cut her eyes at Caleb, hoping that her face didn't betray her fib.

"So, ginger root? I wondered what it was." Marlee held it to her nose. "I kinda like the smell."

Mattie cocked her head. "Kinda strange to find it out there this time of the year. 'specially since it looks like someone dried it to use."

"What would it be used for?" Marlee questioned.

"I makes a tea out of the crushed root for colds and sore throat. Musta fell out of the root woman's basket when she be takin' it to somebody"

"Who's the root woman?" Marlee asked.

"She's a Cherokee woman who lives back in the woods a ways. I been known to get some healin' root from her, time to time. You keep that so's if you get a cold or somethin', it'd be good medicine."

Before Caleb and Marlee could ask any more questions, Mattie took a deep breath and stood up. She brushed the straw from her denim skirt and carefully snuggled the doll. "I need to get on down to your grandmama's house and get her supper goin' 'fore she finds somebody else to do my chores. They's out vistin' church folks today. Y'all come on with me, an' I'll show ya what to do with that ginger root, and maybe we can whip us up a pan of oatmeal cookies."

The three walked across the churchyard with Mattie in the middle, still holding the doll. By the time they were on the road, Mattie was singing again.

"Sweet little Jesus boy, they didn't know who you was...Sweet little Holy Child, they didn't know who you was."

Chapter 17

The sun warmed Caleb's face as he sat beside Marlee on his grandparents' front porch steps. Caleb and Marlee enjoyed a glass of milk and a plate of fresh oatmeal cookies. As promised, Mattie had made a pan of cookies with Caleb and Marlee's help. The cookie dough had felt good between his fingers, especially when he touched Marlee's hands when they kneaded the dough together in the same mixing bowl.

The two friends sat silently, eating their cookies and drinking cool milk. Marlee laid her plate on the steps, stood, and looked at Caleb.

"You know something I just thought?" Marlee had stood as still as when they used to play freeze tag last summer.

Caleb shrugged.

"I bet it was Annabelle who took the doll last year, too. Wonder if she and Abigail brought it back just like they did this time?"

"I guess." Caleb hadn't thought about it either, but he didn't see it mattered much since the mystery had been solved.

"Do you think Annabelle is different because of how she was born, you know, with the veil and all? I mean, she said herself that her mama thought she was special," Marlee said.

"It sure surprised me how much she knew about the

Bible and stuff. Guess she's not as dumb as we thought," Caleb responded.

"I never thought she was dumb! I knew when we saw her in the woods the first time that she had a different look about her. Not a poor look like other people down at the hollow. Maybe it is how she was born, like Mattie said."

"Or maybe her mama treated her differently because of how she was born. You know, read to her from the Bible more. Taught her stuff. Things like that," Caleb said.

Marlee turned to Caleb. "Kinda like Virgil Waters."

"What's Virgil Waters got to do with anythin'?"

"You know. Remember how everyone thought he was dumb, so they made fun of him all the time in school?"

"Well, he did do some dumb things. I mean, putting his head in the fish tank so he could see what the fish saw, now that's kinda dumb."

"Well, yeah, but remember—"

"And the time he had to go to the school nurse because he wanted to see how many dried beans would fit up his nose?" Caleb laughed.

"He was trying to see if the same number would go in both nostrils, that's all."

"And you don't call that dumb?"

Marlee stood in front of Caleb with her arms crossed. "Why do you think Virgil did all that stuff?"

" 'Cause he was dumb."

"No." Marlee shook her head and placed her hands on her sides. " 'Cause some of the boys made fun of him, and he wanted to fit in. That's why."

"Also, remember at the end of the sixth grade when

we got our scores back from one of those intelligence tests?"

"Yeah, they never let us know how we did. Not that I wanted to know." Caleb laughed and took another bite of the cookie.

"Well, I was helping Mrs. Bradley do a *Have A Nice Summer* bulletin board after school, and I overheard her tell Mrs. Thompson that Virgil had the highest scores in the entire sixth grade!"

"Huh? But he was in the Yellow Bird reading group," Caleb said.

"I know. That's what I mean. People treated him like he was dumb, so he acted dumb."

"Well, practice makes perfect!" Caleb laughed.

"And people treated Annabelle differently, so that's how she became different."

"So, you don't think being born with the veil makes you anythin' special?"

"I think that a lot of how you act is because of how you've been treated. If people treat you special, then maybe you'll be a little more special, that's all," Marlee replied.

Mattie opened the screen door. "You two done with your cookies? Miss Marlee? If'n you wanna me ta show you how ta make the ginger root tea, we best get on it. I gotta get supper on 'fore Caleb's grand folks get home from vistin'."

Caleb and Marlee followed Mattie into the kitchen. Caleb pulled up a stool and watched. Mattie had agreed to show Marlee how to prepare the ginger root and store it in a jar just in case someone came down with a cold or cough. Mattie chopped the root into a fine pulp before she dropped it into some simmering water. "Now, we let this steep for a little bit 'fore I pour it up for ya."

Marlee helped Mattie fold some towels while the tea soaked. When the tea was ready, Mattie poured it into a small jar and closed the lid tightly.

"Now, I got a few chores to tend to. Y'all go on out on the porch and let ol' Mattie work. After I be done can yall stay here 'til your grandma and grandpa get back from vistin'? I'll need to get on to my house. Lots of chores waitin' on me there, for sho!"

"Sure, we can stay," Caleb answered. He poured himself another glass of milk and snatched a cookie from the plate on the table. Marlee was deep in thought when they returned to the porch. She held the warm jar of tea to her cheek.

"I think Annabelle was getting the ginger root for Abigail. She must be sick."

"What makes you think she's sick?"

"Well, she was getting it for somebody. Maybe Abigail got a cold from being outside on Christmas Eve night. I just wonder if Annabelle knows how to make it." Marlee began twisting her hair and staring across the road into the woods.

Caleb set his milk glass down hard on the porch. "Oh, no! You're not thinkin' what I think you're thinkin'."

"I want to take this to Annabelle." Marlee held the jar to the sky and carefully studied the amber liquid.

Caleb jumped up on the porch steps. "There's no way we're goin' down to Smoky's place. That's crazy! We shouldn't be goin' back to the hollow again. We were lucky last time you wanted to go there, remember—your bike—and Smoky? Besides, Annabelle obviously knows how to use the ginger root to make tea. Why do you think she was takin' it out of that buried box? No. We can't be goin' back down there." As the words spilled out of Caleb's mouth, he knew one thing for certain: he was going back to the hollow to Smoky's place no matter how much he protested.

Chapter 18

The following morning, Caleb pulled his bike into the church parking lot. Marlee was already there holding the small jar of ginger root tea Mattie had prepared. Earlier that morning, while her mother was getting dressed upstairs, Marlee heated the tea in a pan and poured it back into the jar. She wrapped the tea in a cloth, stuck it into her coat pocket, and headed out the door. A note on the counter simply read, *Meeting Caleb at the church. Back soon.*

****

"Okay, what's the plan?" Marlee asked.

"The plan? The plan is to have your head checked. I still think this is crazy."

"I want to get this ginger tea to Annabelle. Are you with me, or am I going by myself?"

Caleb sighed loudly, tightened his lips, and stared where the nativity scene once stood. He looked intently at Marlee and shook his head.

"Well…I'm not letting you go down there alone."

"My hero!" Marlee responded with a hint of sarcasm.

"How will you know where the girls are, anyway? What if they're in the house with Smoky? What then? He'll just tell us to 'git' and sic the hounds on us."

"I think they stay in the smokehouse where we saw Annabelle. The last one is back in the woods.

Remember?"

"Of course, I remember."

Marlee stuffed the jar of ginger tea into the coat pocket, leaned on her handlebars, and studied the ground, thinking. "Okay, how 'bout this idea? You knock on Smoky's door, and while you are talking to him—

"Whoa, whoa! I'm not doin' that! No siree!" Caleb shook his head in total defiance of Marlee's plan. "Let's ride down to the bridge and figure this out from there. Albert might show up here any minute, and I don't want him to know anythin' about this crazy plan."

****

It was a chilly day but the sun was bright, lifting the two friends' spirits as they coasted down Cane Creek Road. By the time they got to the bridge, they were feeling better about their mission of mercy. The bubbling voices of the creek cautioned them to rethink their mission while the road to the hollow looked as bleak and threatening as they had remembered. They parked on the bridge and stared down the dark road. Neither spoke.

Then Caleb turned to Marlee. "Okay, if we are doin' this, here's the plan. When we get close to Smoky's place, we hide our bikes in the brush and cut through the woods 'til we see the smokehouse. That way, we won't be seen if anybody comes down the road."

"Good. I can do that." Marlee shook her head, agreeing. "Then what?"

Caleb shrugged. "That's all I got. We'll figure it out from there."

They dodged the tire ruts and mud holes and fought the dirt road that twisted into the hollow. Eventually, they saw the turn-off to Smoky's place. Caleb pulled their bicycles across a ditch and pushed them into a thicket of evergreen briars, concealing them from the road.

Struggling through the underbrush, they climbed the steep hill toward the smokehouse. Caleb helped Marlee untangle a stretch of smilax sticker vines from her jeans. He then took her hand and led her up the hill. When they stopped, Caleb surveyed the area. He pointed to a grove of trees in the distance. "Let's get over to that stand of pines. It will be easier 'cause there won't be much undergrowth and we can see better." Caleb had learned a few tricks while trudging through the forest with his grandpa, scouting out good hunting spots.

Once they were under the pines at the top of the ridgeline, Smoky's place came into view. Caleb scanned the property and saw no sign of Smoky or his truck. "We're in luck, it looks like Smokys not home."

"I wonder if Annabelle is with him?" Marlee replied.

"There's the smokehouse." Caleb pointed through the trees at the little cabin nestled deep against the mountain. From this vantage point, Caleb could see light escaping through a small window on the side of the little house. "It looks like a candle is burnin' in there."

Marlee pushed some pine branches aside and peered down the mountainside. "How do we get down there?"

"Let's follow this deer trail to the back of the smokehouse. That way we won't be seen if Smoky comes home."

Marlee followed Caleb's lead, and soon they stood in the rear of the tiny smokehouse. A thin whiff of wood smoke trailed from the small chimney and drifted across the tree tops.

Caleb stepped back and let Marlee go first. After all, this was her mission. He had gotten her this far; now it was up to her. Caleb was there to see that nothing went wrong, or so he hoped. Marlee walked tenderly to the small door and knocked. "Annabelle? Abigail? Anyone in there?"

She gently pulled on the smokehouse door and peeked inside. Caleb brushed past her and stepped in first, just in case one of the hound dogs was in there. The house was smaller than his bedroom, but rather large for a smokehouse. The low ceiling of exposed rafters was still tethered by rotten twine where hams once dangled from the rough-hewn logs. The house hadn't been used for smoking for quite a while, yet the red clay floor still had a slight greasy feel from tallow drippings.

The only light came from one thick white candle on a rustic table and a slight glow from a small wood-burning stove in the far corner. As Caleb's eyes adjusted to the dim light in the room, he noticed a woven straw pallet on the dirt floor. A crude mattress, stuffed with what seemed to be corn shucks, lay on the red clay floor. Abigail rested on the make-shift pallet. The young girl was covered from her neck down with several burlap bags. Annabelle sat on a hickory stump beside her sister but jumped immediately to her feet when Caleb entered the smokehouse.

Marlee stepped up beside Caleb. "Hi, Annabelle. Remember us? Marlee and Caleb?"

Annabelle was silent. The only sound was the crackle of pine sticks in the stove and a muffled cough from Abigail.

Annabelle finally spoke. "I 'member you. What y'all doin' here? Annabelle moved behind the small table; her eyes were wide. "I done put the baby back."

Abigail had pulled the burlap across her face. Only the top of her head showed.

"That's okay. Don't be afraid. We came here because we found this ginger root you dropped in the woods and thought you might need it…for somebody." Marlee looked at the little girl on the floor. "Is Abigail sick?"

"Did the angel send ya here?" Anabelle stayed behind the table.

Caleb sent a questioning look to Marlee.

"I…we don't know who that is?" Marlee reached into her coat pocket and pulled out the jar of ginger tea. She could still feel the warmth of the small jar wrapped in a dishcloth. "We brought you and Abigail some ginger root tea to help if you have a cold. Mattie made it for us. She's the woman who—"

"I know'd who she is," Annabelle interrupted.

Marlee stepped toward Annabelle and placed the wrapped jar on the table. "Here. It's still warm." Marlee smiled at the little girl lying on the pallet. "Hi, Abigail. My name is Marlee. Are you feeling poorly?"

Abigail pulled the burlap off her mouth. "Baby! Baby Jesus!"

Marlee grinned and looked at Caleb, still standing guard by the door. "Yes, Abigail. You remember the doll?" Abigail just smiled and covered her mouth with the burlap.

Marlee reached into her pocket and took out two peppermint sticks. She turned toward Annabelle. "These are for you and Abigail."

Both girls' eyes widened when they saw the candy sticks. "I remember you liked peppermint." Marlee laid them gently on the table.

The sound of hound dogs bawling startled Caleb. He opened the door slightly and peered toward the cabin. Smoky's truck had just pulled into the yard. "We gotta go!" Caleb demanded, keeping his eyes on Smoky unloading some bags from the truck bed.

"Annabelle, will you give Abigail some of this tea? It will help her to get well." Marlee backed away from the table toward where Caleb was standing.

"I can do jus' that. I do it when the angel brings it." Annabelle nodded as she spoke.

"Well, I'm no angel. But—"

Caleb pulled the sleeve of Marlee's coat and whispered. "Smoky went inside. We hav'ta go *now*!"

The smokehouse door closed as Caleb and Marlee ran toward the cover of the pines. Caleb pulled Marlee along the trail in almost a full run. They ran as fast as possible down the trail, skipping over roots and dodging pine limbs. Neither spoke as they found their bikes, yanked them out of the brush, and rode out of the hollow as fast as their legs would push the pedals.

When they coasted onto the bridge, they stopped to catch their breath.

"That was a close one!" Caleb exclaimed.

Marlee smiled at Caleb. "Remember earlier when I said you were my hero? Well, I meant it." She leaned over and kissed Caleb's cheek before taking off down Cane Creek Road. "Race ya to the church!"

Caleb pushed off and peddled with all his might. His face was as red as a tomato, but it wasn't because of the cold wind. Soon, he was riding beside Marlee as they rounded the curve and saw the church in the distance.

They slowed their bikes, and Marlee pointed at an

orange object floating above the church steeple. "Do you see that? What is it?"

Caleb pedaled faster and turned into the church parking lot. Albert stood in the field beside the church holding his arms above his head and guiding a kite away from the steeple.

Marlee stopped beside Caleb, who was already off his bike and walking toward Albert.

"Hey, Caleb, remember our deal." Marlee held up her pinky finger. "Don't say a word about…you know."

Caleb nodded in agreement and then waved at Albert.

"Hey, you two. I've been waiting for ya. Look at the cool kite I got for Christmas!"

The breeze held the string taut while the kite soared above their heads. Marlee ran beside Albert. 'That's a beautiful kite, Albert. Can I try?"

Albert blushed. "Sure! Let me show you." He handed the plastic piece to Marlee and explained the parts.

"This is the spindle, and the line is called a tether. It's connected to a bridle which holds the kite."

Marlee held the spindle and felt the pull of the kite. "Wow, this is so neat! I didn't know a kite had all these parts. You're so smart!"

Albert beamed with pride. "I just read the instructions, that's all."

For the next hour, the three friends took turns flying the kite and talking about how they would spend their last days of Christmas break.

Chapter 19

Caleb closed his eyes and willed himself to sleep. He tossed under his covers as the day's events marched across the backs of his eyelids. In his mind, he replayed the trip to the hollow to see Annabelle and Abigail. The memory of the dimly lit smokehouse and the smell of rancid tallow filled his head. The faces of the two young girls haunted him. Why do they have to live like they do? The things Mattie had said that afternoon brought up many questions. Was it possible that Annabelle could see things differently than other people just because of how she was born?

He rolled over and closed his eyes, but sleep still eluded him. Then Caleb remembered making cookies. He could hear the laughter from his grandparents' kitchen as Mattie told story after story while Caleb and Marlee licked the traces of dough from the spoon and mixing bowl. The aroma of cookies baked in the oven filled the room, and images of Marlee's wide, bright eyes and dimpled cheeks danced through his mind. He touched his cheek where Marlee had kissed and called him "her hero." He again felt the blood rush to his face.

Caleb thought about Mattie leaving his grandparents' house that afternoon. He heard the screen door slam behind Mattie as she stepped onto the back porch. She was barely off the porch steps before she broke into song. Her voice trailed off when she turned the corner of the house. Caleb rolled over on his side, and the thought struck him: Mattie never used the front door. Even when her ride was on the street, she always came and went through the back door.

He lay on his back, tucked the covers to his chin, and stared at the dancing lines on the ceiling. The shadow of the red maple tree in front of the street light reached across his room like skeleton hands opening and closing with each breeze. Caleb remembered lying in bed last winter, with his eyes shut tight, trying not to get a glimpse of the ghostly silhouette. The hands had seemed to be reaching out for him, fingers stretching through the darkness. But tonight, his eyes followed the finger-like branches as he thought about the afternoon in the kitchen with Marlee.

He reached out from his covers and traced the limbs of the maple tree across his ceiling. As his eyelids finally became heavy, his mind branched into as many thoughts as the forks in the tree's shadow. In this state of near slumber, he wasn't in control of the images in his mind. Caleb was only a bystander.

In his dream, he saw Annabelle and Abigail by the manger on Christmas Eve, placing Marlee's doll carefully in the hay. Then the image of Abigail lying on the corn-shuck mattress in the smokehouse crowded his mind. He could see the smokehouse with the door slightly ajar. His daddy was perched atop the smokehouse wearing his carpenter's apron.

"We need your help to fix this." Caleb opened his toolbox and removed his hammer, but it faded into the mist, and he was left looking at his empty hand.

He heard his father's voice, "Good job, Caleb." Then he saw Marlee and Mattie in the kitchen making cookies and heard Mattie telling tales of the sea islands where she was born. He heard Marlee's voice say, "You are my hero!"

Suddenly, he was back in the woods near the smokehouse. Everywhere he looked he saw smoke, the woods full like a deep morning fog. He could see someone approaching through the thick haze. His stride was familiar, and he carried a turkey by the neck.

"There sure is a lot of smoke in this world," his grandpa said. He handed the bird to Mattie, who turned and walked into the haze singing, *Sweet little Jesus boy...they didn't know who you was...*

In his dream, the smokehouse door creaked slowly open. In the thick smoke that surrounded him, he could see a solitary candle on an old wooden table inside the building. The candle's brilliant light seemed to chase the smoke away.

As he approached the smokehouse, he stopped. Annabelle was sitting on the steps rocking a doll in her arms.

"Ain't no baby yet," she said, looking straight at Caleb with bright blue eyes.

****

The pounding got louder and louder. It came from everywhere. Caleb opened his eyes and gazed at the shadows of the maple tree across the ceiling. He heard footsteps and then muffled voices. The door to his bedroom creaked open.

"Caleb, are you awake?" his mother said in a hushed voice.

"Uh, yes Ma'am, I think so. What's going on?" Caleb leaned on one elbow, trying to adjust his eyes to the light spilling in from the hallway.

His mother slipped into the room and turned on the bedside lamp. Caleb shielded his eyes from the light. The wind-up clock on his nightstand said it was 11:30.

"Mr. Patterson is here. There's been a fire tonight."

"Fire? Where?" Caleb bolted straight up in his bed, now fully awake.

"At Smoky Pruitt's place. Mr. Patterson's nephew is with the volunteer fire department. They've been working for a while, trying to keep the fire from spreading into the woods. He sent Mr. Patterson over here because Mrs. Patterson told her family at Christmas about y'all seeing Annabelle and Abigail Christmas Eve. They can't find any signs of the girls or Smoky. Mr. Patterson was wondering if you and Marlee might have an idea where the girls could be. We're getting a few things together to take down there."

"They stay in one of the old smokehouses, I think. The one set back in the woods a ways. We saw Annabelle there when we went to get the hams." Caleb didn't want to break his pinky swear he had made with Marlee but the girls might be in trouble. "Have they checked in there?"

More voices sounded from the front porch and car doors opened and banged shut. "Who else is here?" Caleb pulled his covers back and stepped, barefoot, onto the cold wood floor.

His mother walked to the door and looked out into the hallway. "I hear Margaret, and it sounds like Marlee is with them, too. I'll go see."

At that, Caleb snatched on his blue jeans, tennis shoes, and red checkered shirt. He quickly ran a comb through his hair and met them as they were coming in from the porch.

"I'm not sure I want you kids down there. It could be dangerous or somebody might be layin' up dead, you never know," Marlee's mother said.

"But Mamma, we've *got* to find Annabelle and Abigail. Caleb and I can show you where they might be." Marlee grabbed Caleb's arm and pulled him next to her for support.

"As far as we know they're with their daddy somewhere," Marlee's mother said.

Mr. Patterson stuck his head in the door and waved his arm at his wife. "C'mon! We need to get down there if we're gonna be any help a 'tall."

"I've got some sandwiches here. Those girls might be starving." Caleb's mother scurried from the kitchen with a rolled-down paper sack.

Marlee's mother pointed to the Patterson's car in the driveway, "I threw in a couple of Marlee's old coats in case they don't have anythin'."

Caleb's dad came from the bedroom with some flashlights. "Okay, kids, you can go, but stay in the car until I tell you. You hear?"

With that said, Caleb and Marlee scampered down the steps and jumped into the back seat of the Austins' car before their parents could change their minds.

Chapter 20

Caleb rubbed the car window with his coat sleeve to clear the fog as his dad's Buick slowed and crossed the old bridge to the hollow. Marlee leaned over Caleb's shoulder to see down the dark dirt road. The scent of her freshly washed hair filled Caleb with each breath. He had often caught a whiff of this fragrance when he sat behind her in the Sunday School assembly. He hadn't thought anything of it then, but now, with her face just inches from his cheek, he found it difficult to concentrate on the woods beyond.

"I sure hope they find those poor little girls," Caleb's mother said from the front seat.

"They have some competent men searching right now. I'm sure they'll find them. They're most likely with Smoky. The girls might not have even been home when the fire started," Caleb's dad responded confidently.

They rode past the house where Caleb and Marlee had seen the wake days before when they rode their bikes into the hollow. The drive that led to the Pruitts' place was blocked by a fire truck. Caleb's dad had to pull off to the side and park.

The flashing light of the fire engine darted from under its globe atop the truck and struck the mountainside like a red sword slashing the darkness. Caleb couldn't see the house from where he was sitting, but a massive plume of smoke billowed into the night sky, catching the light from the engine and reflecting the embers below. The smell of the burning wood seeped into the car.

"Remember, y'all stay right here," Caleb's dad ordered when Marlee's father's truck pulled up behind his car. The two men met up and walked across the road to the fire engine where Mr. Patterson's nephew stood, talking into his hand-held radio.

Caleb turned to watch a few other cars that had attempted to drive onto the road behind them. A fireman jerked his red-coned flashlight for them to go back the way they had come. Caleb sat up tall in the seat and watched the cars maneuver to leave the road. He felt special, like a secret agent called in for an assignment.

Bright dashes of light shot through the woods as men with high-powered flashlights probed through the mountain laurel and pine thickets. The smoke had permeated the mountainside so the light scattered in diffused beams. Caleb realized they were searching for Smoky and the girls. He thought of the trail he and Marlee had used earlier that day. Should he tell someone about the trail to the smokehouse? He glanced at Marlee but didn't say anything.

Mrs. Patterson stuck her head in the window beside Caleb's mother. "They say it's spreading into the woods and up the mountainside."

"Why can't we go with Daddy?" Marlee whined.

"Your daddy will say when you can get out, just hold yer horses."

At that moment, Mrs. Patterson's nephew walked over to the car. He tipped his fire hat to the ladies, bent down, and looked through the back seat window that Caleb had rolled down.

"Marlee, I heard you know something about these girls."

"We think they sometimes stay in one of the smokehouses." Caleb cut his eyes at Marlee and remembered their pact not to tell anyone they were here earlier. "Caleb and I can show you." Marlee scrambled for the door handle.

But Marlee's mother planted both her hands on the car door. "It might be best for you to tell them and let these men do their job."

The fireman turned. "Aunt Margaret, we might find them faster if the kids could point out this smokehouse. Since we can't find Mr. Pruitt, they could be here alone. Don't worry, I'll watch after them."

Marlee didn't waste any time. She sprang out of the car next to her cousin, and Caleb jumped from the backseat after her. Caleb's mother protested, but it was too late. Caleb and Marlee had already run to the head of the trail.

"You have to go on this trail to see the smokehouses," Marlee instructed, pointing up the path. She immediately took the lead with Caleb beside her. Both of their dads followed behind.

The group paused in front of the small, A-framed cold house where the Christmas hams had hung a few weeks ago. From there, Caleb could see the burning house for the first time. The skeleton-like framework glowed through the dense smoke and steam. The whoosh from the hoses and the drone of the pump from the engine filled his ears. Caleb had never seen a house on fire. Caleb's grandpa had burned a large pile of old lumber once last year, but that was the biggest fire Caleb had ever witnessed.

Muffled commands came from the direction of the house as the firemen in yellow rubber raincoats rushed around the building, continuing to douse the structure with water.

The flames were dying, but small blazes still erupted throughout the charred house. Most of the roof and one wall had collapsed, and the upsurge of smoke lifted sparkling ashes high into the cold, early morning air.

"Wonder where Smoky is?" As they paused on the hill, Mr. Patterson turned and gazed down the hill in the direction of the burning house.

"We haven't seen any signs of him," his nephew replied. "The chief seems to think that the fire started from the old woodstove or maybe a fireplace in the house, so he may not even have been home."

"I don't see the hound dogs anywhere. Maybe Smoky took 'em coon huntin'," Caleb observed.

"That's some helpful information," the fireman replied. He activated his walkie-talkie and communicated with the fire chief.

Caleb's dad patted Caleb on the shoulder and turned to the fireman. "I doubt the girls would be coon hunting, so, they must still be somewhere around."

Marlee stepped ahead of the group. "Right down this trail, you'll see several smokehouses. The one Annabelle plays in is by itself, back in the trees a bit." At that, one of the firemen aimed his flashlight in the direction she was pointing.

Smoke floated like tattered ribbons through the light beam, and the first house came into view. Two other buildings were faintly visible beyond, but the smoke became thicker the closer they got to the little house.

"That's it, right over there." Marlee pointed. They

could see light escaping through the cracks in the mud packing and slipping out from underneath the crude slatted door.

"Someone's in there! Marlee exclaimed. She ran up the trail away from the group and disappeared into a swirling cloud of smoke.

"Marlee! Marlee! Stay right there," Mr. Patterson screamed.

Down the slope, to the right of the group, the forest was ablaze. Glowing embers spewed through the tops of the trees. The breeze was now blowing stronger, igniting the dry brush with flaming tongues that licked their way up the mountainside toward them. The smoke had almost completely obscured the flashlight beams, blanketing the entire path. Caleb and the men coughed and stuck their faces under their coat collars.

Up the mountainside, a pack of hound dogs bawled.

"That might be Smoky's hounds!" Caleb's voice was muffled. He had pulled his coat collar across his mouth.

Mr. Patterson frantically called for Marlee. "Which way did she go?" he cried, crashing through the thick brush, unable to see even a foot ahead.

"Hold up, Uncle Melvin. We'll find her. Just get yourself low to the ground and stay put."

Marlee's cousin shone his light in the direction he thought she had run, but the smoke was too dense, obscuring the path and making it impossible to see anything. The cry of the dogs spilled down the mountainside while frantic voices shouted along the trail behind them. All the while, the smoke thickened and ashes rained.

Caleb could now feel the heat of the fire racing up

the slope. He had to do something. He was the only one who knew the trail.

"Caleb!" His father screamed when his son disappeared into the smoke.

"I know what I'm doing! I'll be right back!" Caleb wasn't sure if they heard, but he couldn't wait for help. He bent low and groped across the forest floor, falling to his hands and knees. The acrid taste of the ashes burned his throat, and every breath felt like he had inhaled his grandpa's smoker.

The blaze, by now, had reached the treetops directly overhead, and ashes from the scorching pine needles showered the area. In the light of the fire, he could see the smokehouse a few yards ahead. In the middle of the path, a dark bundle lay.

It was Marlee. She was on her side with her knees pulled to her chest and her face pushed deep into her coat.

"Marlee! Get up, we've gotta get outta here, now!" At that second, a fiery limb crashed onto the trail behind them, blocking any escape route. Caleb thrust his hands under Marlee's arms and yanked her to her feet. The reflection of the flames danced in her eyes. Terror washed over her face. Caleb pushed her down the trail toward the smokehouse. He grabbed the old rusty nail on the door and jerked it open. The two stumbled onto the dirt floor, coughing and gasping for breath. He didn't hear the door close behind him.

From outside, Caleb and Marlee heard the muffled sounds of urgent voices in the distance and the crash of burning limbs, but their attention was focused on the figures in the dark corner. Annabelle and Abigail huddled in the back of the smokehouse. The girls wore dirty, torn nightgowns and no coats. High-topped leather shoes swallowed their tiny feet.

Caleb watched Annabelle brush the hair from Abigail's crying eyes, and with calm determination, she quoted a Psalm he had heard his grandmother read many times. "God is our refuge an' stren'th, a very pres'nt hep in trouble."

"Y'all don't be scared now. We're goin' to get you outta here." Caleb heard his words, but they sounded like they came from somewhere far away. He could see the amber glow of flames through the cracks in the smokehouse wall when he rose from the floor. He had no idea what to do next. Marlee lay on the dirt floor, coughing and sobbing. Caleb knew that he needed to get all of them out of there.

Abigail clutched Annabelle's gown with her tiny fist and stared deep into her sister's eyes, seeming to shut out all the chaos around her.

Suddenly, the door burst open, and Marlee screamed. A column of smoke rushed in, followed by several bawling hounds and Smoky Pruitt. He had a bandanna tied around his head, covering his face like a train robber in an old western movie. Tossing his shotgun on the mattress, he scooped up his daughters, one under each arm. He turned to Caleb, who had backed against the wall, keeping his distance from the maze of frightened hunting dogs bounding around the tiny room and bawling.

"Git outta here rat now!" Smoky yelled.

Caleb thought he was hollering at the dogs until Smoky grabbed Caleb's shoulder and shoved him toward the door. "This place is gonna burn like a dry twig any minute. Now git!"

Caleb seized Marlee's arm and dragged her out the door into the midst of a noxious cloud of smoke. After him, Smoky charged. He carried the girls under his arms like two sacks of potatoes, their feet dangling inches from the ground. Smoke and ash had completely enveloped the path, and a burning pine limb blocked the way. Blazing limbs overhead promised to fall any minute.

"Go on up th' hill that-a-way!" With his face still covered by the bandanna, Smoky jerked his head for them to go into the brush. Caleb crashed through the thicket, knocking briars away with one hand and pulling Marlee with the other. Smoky, only a few feet behind, followed his lead. They climbed higher until they were on another trail. Crying, Marlee collapsed onto the forest floor. Caleb looked below and saw the mountainside ablaze with thick billows of smoke that swirled into the air. The wind behind them kept the smoke rolling on the old smokehouse trail like an ebb tide. A second later, he saw the roof of the smokehouse crash and burst into flames.

Smoky let go of Annabelle and thrust Abigail into Caleb's arms. "Y'all git on down th' trail." He pointed to where Caleb had left his father and the rest of the group. "I gotta hep 'em git outta there 'fore they all burn up." He ripped the bandanna from his face and stuck it in Caleb's hand. "Here, wear this." Then, he and the dogs disappeared into the smoke. Caleb looked at the old red bandanna, the thin cloth that had protected Smoky when he and his dogs had entered the cabin.

With a renewed sense of mission, Caleb held Abigail with one arm and tugged at Marlee's hand. "Get up, Marlee! You have to help Annabelle. C'mon, we have to go now!"

Weakly, Marlee stood up, coughing, her face whiter than the curled ashes snowing from the burning treetops. Annabelle reached up and grasped Marlee's hand. The two girls stared at each other as the veil of smoke blanketed the mountainside. When Caleb looked at the girls, he saw more than frightened eyes and soot-covered faces. The things that separated them were no longer important. No creek divided their worlds. No social class determined the way they should act. This was survival. The only thing that mattered was getting out alive.

Caleb lifted Abigail and hugged her tightly to him, covering her mouth with the bandanna. Annabelle stepped out front, pulled Marlee with one hand, and clutched the other close to her chest. The children ran through the winding switchbacks and along the ridgeline for what seemed like hours but, in fact, were only minutes.

The trail opened to a sea of emergency vehicles. Red and blue lights cut across the faces of the children as they burst out of the woods. From the back of an ambulance, Marlee's mother jumped out and screamed,

"Here they are!"

Suddenly, there was a flurry of activity, with the mamas hugging and kissing the children. The rescue squad workers shined flashlights in their faces and checked them for burns and smoke inhalation. An emergency worker kneeled on a blanket and attended to an injured fireman. Marlee fell to her knees beside them. Firemen immediately laid her on a blanket and put an oxygen mask over her face.

Still holding tight to Caleb, Abigail buried her face in the collar of his coat. A woman rescue worker spoke quietly to the child and, in a few minutes, was able to take her from Caleb. Annabelle stood beside Marlee and clutched what appeared to be a Bible close to her when a woman rescue worker returned and took her by the hand. Through the window of the ambulance, Caleb could see workers placing a stethoscope on Abigail's chest.

Caleb leaned against the side of an ambulance and drank a cup of orange juice a worker had given him. His mother stood beside him and rubbed his face with a wet cloth.

"I'm okay, Mama." He gently pushed her arm away from his face. "Where's Daddy?"

"Right here, son." He walked around the back of the ambulance, holding the same type of cup they had given Caleb. "I was checking on Marlee's father. He was in pretty bad shape but seems to be doing fine now that he got some oxygen."

Caleb's dad towered in front of his son, looking down at him but not saying a word. Caleb looked sheepishly into his cup. "Sorry, Daddy, for running off like that. I guess I messed everything up."

There was a long pause, and then his dad laid his hand on Caleb's shoulders. "Son, look at me. Sometimes, a man has to go with his gut. You did a good job. I'm proud of you. Because of you, these girls got out alive."

Caleb's dad took a drink of juice and shook his head. He gave a nervous chuckle. "Those hound dogs sure saved our lives. We couldn't tell which way to go when the fire raced up the mountain until they showed up. We just followed them right on out."

"What about Smoky?" Caleb asked.

"Smoky? Was he there? We never saw him. Why, did you?"

Caleb looked surprised. "Yes. He got us out of the smokehouse and took us to another trail up the mountain. He said he had to help y'all get out. Then he left."

Without a word, Caleb's father walked straight to Marlee's cousin, standing by the edge of the woods, shouting orders to the men on the slope below him. Caleb couldn't hear what they were saying, but they kept pointing to the trail entrance. Several firemen with masks ran back into the woods as Marlee's cousin yelled more orders to the firefighters down the hillside.

A rescue worker talked to Caleb's dad and then walked over to Caleb and his mother. "Ma'am," he said, politely tipping his hat. "We'd like to take the children to the Asheville Regional Emergency Room to be checked out. It's simply a precaution, nothing to worry about."

"The hospital? You want to take them there?" She reached for Caleb and squeezed his hand tightly. "I don't know, I mean…" She looked around nervously. Marlee had been taken to the other ambulance with Annabelle and Abigail. Caleb could see them through the window, drinking their juice.

"It's simply a precaution. I'm sure they're fine, but it's always best to get a doctor's opinion," the rescue worker said in a soothing voice. On the pocket of his soot-covered uniform, a name tag that said *Strickland* in silver letters was pinned above a red cross.

Caleb's father now joined them beside the ambulance. "Joshua, they want to take them to the hospital. To the emergency room."

"I know. It's okay, Sarah. I just checked on Marlee and the Pruitt girls. They're doin' fine. We'll ride with Melvin and Margaret and meet them there."

"But what about Smoky?" Caleb interrupted.

"They haven't found him yet. They think they've stopped the fire from spreadin', so maybe he's around somewhere."

"I'm riding in here with Caleb." Caleb's mom was already climbing into the back of the ambulance.

"Mama, I'm fine. I don't need—"

"Now you hush. There's no way you're riding in an ambulance to the hospital without me." She plopped down and folded her arms. Caleb knew there was no use arguing.

Caleb's dad looked at Caleb, shrugged, and then turned to his wife. "Melvin and I will meet you there. We're gonna stop by and let Henry know what's goin' on." He leaned into the ambulance and gave his wife a gentle kiss on the cheek. "It's goin' to be fine."

Caleb's mother sat on a trunk that served both as a bench and for storing equipment. Caleb started to climb into the ambulance behind his mother when he saw something on the ground in the middle of the road. It was Smoky's bandanna. Caleb stooped and picked it up. Then he carefully folded it and put it deep into his pocket.

Chapter 21

Caleb and Marlee were released from the Asheville hospital early the following day. Their parents had checked them out, but before leaving, Caleb and Marlee stopped by the nurse's desk and asked about Annabelle and Abigail. No one at the hospital would give them any information about the two girls' conditions.

On the way home, Caleb's dad said that the fire was finally extinguished, but not before burning Smoky's cabin, all of the smokehouses, and close to twenty acres of the surrounding forest.

****

In the following days, life slowly returned to its regular routine. School had started, and Caleb and Marlee were occupied with homework, chores, and an occasional bike ride to Harper's store. Still, two weeks had passed, and they had no updates on Annabelle and Abigail. However, early the following week, a Henderson County deputy sheriff contacted Caleb and Marlee's parents and arranged an interview at Caleb's house.

The afternoon of the meeting, their parents sat in the Austins' den talking while Caleb and Marlee waited impatiently on the front porch.

"I don't understand why they can't tell us anything about Annabelle and Abigail," Caleb said as he paced the floorboards.

"I sure hope they're alright. I mean, we are okay, so I figure they are too," Marlee reasoned. She was standing by the porch banister, watching for the deputy to arrive.

Caleb stood beside her. "When your cousin called, did he know anything at all about the girls...or the fire?"

Marlee shook her head. "He just told my mother that the fire was out and they were still investigating everything. Then he told her about Smoky."

"I hope that...well...they don't think we had anythin' to do with the fire," Caleb spoke quietly, leaning into Marlee. "I mean, we were just there earlier that day. You took the ginger root to Abigail, and Smoky came and went in his house, remember?"

Marlee glanced toward the door and whispered, "Of course I remember!" She held up her little finger. "Our secret, right?"

"Sure. But I wonder if they talked to Annabelle and if she said anything about us comin' to see them."

Marlee shook her head. "Look, all we did was go to Annabelle's smokehouse. That's all. We had nothing to do with the fire."

Caleb nodded but didn't speak.

When the patrol car pulled into the Austins' driveway, Caleb and Marlee ran to meet the deputy. They stood patiently beside the sheriff's cruiser while he made a call on his car radio. Caleb and Marlee's parents came out on the porch.

"Kids, y'all come on up here. We will talk inside." Caleb's daddy walked down the steps and introduced himself to the officer. Moments later, they sat in Caleb's living room, answering questions from the deputy. Caleb and Marlee's parents were present, but the officer directed his questions to the kids.

"Our children had nothing to do with this fire." Marlee's mother had made this comment for the third time. The deputy patiently reminded Mrs. Patterson that the children were not in any trouble, but anytime there was a death, an investigation followed.

Mr. Patterson patted his wife on the shoulder. "Just let the officer get the story from Marlee and Caleb. Everything is fine."

Caleb glanced at Marlee as he watched the deputy flip the pages of his notepad.

"The fire seems to have started in Mr. Pruitt's cabin. It appears that a burning log may have rolled out of the fireplace onto the floor," the sheriff's deputy informed. "But I can tell you for sure that Annabelle and Abigail are well and in the safe custody of the social services department."

"But do they know about Smoky…I mean Mr. Pruitt, their daddy?" Marlee asked.

"I'm sure the social worker has explained the situation to the girls." The officer wrote something in his notepad and continued to ask Caleb and Marlee about the events of that night. After they had explained everything that had happened on the mountain, the deputy stood and placed his pad in his front pocket.

"I'm just glad you two are okay. I'm sure the entire ordeal was a frightening experience. And Caleb, I wouldn't be surprised if there's a commendation coming to you for your bravery that night."

Caleb didn't respond. He stared at his feet as the deputy thanked his parents and left.

"Wouldn't that be something? You might get a certificate or, who knows, maybe even a medal for bravery!" Caleb's mother patted her son on his shoulder and walked toward the kitchen. "I'll put on a pot of coffee."

Mrs. Patterson followed while the men recanted the events of the night of the fire. Caleb quietly slipped out to the front porch and sat in the swing. Marlee came to the porch and eased onto the swing beside Caleb. The two friends sat silent, staring at the woods beyond the yard.

Eventually, Caleb turned to Marlee with a troubled expression. "I don't want no medal or anythin'."

"But Caleb, you saved Anabelle and Abigail...and me!" Marlee touched Caleb's arm and smiled.

"It was Smoky, you know that. You were there. He showed us how to get outta the woods. Without him, maybe none of us would've made it. He's the one who deserves a medal if anybody does."

Marlee shook her head. "*You* got us out, Caleb, not Smoky. But you know what hurts my heart? Those little girls lost their daddy. I know he was crazy and sometimes mean, but he was still their daddy. That's what bothers me the most."

Marlee lay her head on Caleb's shoulder while they enjoyed the quiet and felt the swing gently sway. Caleb smiled.

****

The high school auditorium was packed when the mayor approached the podium.

"Citizens of Fletcher, welcome. Thank you for coming out for this special event. Tonight, we recognize several of our brave citizens within our community for service above and beyond. As you know, a couple of months ago, there was a devastating fire in the mountains surrounding our town. Unfortunately, lives and property were lost during this tragedy, but due to the heroic efforts of our brave firefighters and citizens, lives were also saved."

Caleb sat on the stage next to Marlee's cousin and two other firemen he recognized from the night of the fire. He scanned the sea of faces in the audience. Marlee and her family sat in the front row with Caleb's mother and father. He spotted his grandpa and grandma a few rows back.

The mayor continued. "One of our young citizens was responsible for saving several lives that night." He turned and motioned for Caleb to come to the podium and stand beside him. Caleb shyly walked across the stage and stood next to the mayor.

"Caleb Austin, because of your courage and selfless acts the night of the tragic fire in the mountains around Fletcher, the city council has voted to award you our highest citizenship award for bravery." The mayor handed Caleb a certificate and placed a medal around his neck. He then shook Caleb's hand. "Thank you, young man. It's a pleasure to have you as a citizen of Fletcher."

Caleb choked a faint "thank you" and returned to his seat.

When the ceremony concluded, Caleb's family and friends surrounded him, patting his back and congratulating him. Caleb mustered a slight smile, but he was unsure how he felt. He was overwhelmed. He just wanted to go home and get out of his Sunday clothes. He loosened his tie and moved slowly toward the door.

Marlee joined Caleb, and they strolled outside the auditorium, where they paused on the steps and waited for their families. Caleb was ready to leave, but his parents had stalled inside, talking to several church members.

Suddenly, Bobby Henderson sidled up beside Caleb.

"Let's have a look at that medal." He reached and lifted it off Caleb's chest and turned it over. Caleb braced himself but wasn't in the mood for a fight, especially in front of Marlee, his family, and half the town of Fletcher.

Bobby let go of the medal and gave a sly grin. "How does it feel to be a big hero?"

"I wouldn't know 'cause I'm not a hero," Caleb snapped. He slid the medal over his head and stuffed it deep into the pocket of his Sunday pants.

Marlee took Caleb's arm, leaned in, and kissed his cheek. "He's *my* hero!"

With that, Bobby's smirk fell. He nodded his head and quietly walked away. Caleb blushed.

Chapter 22

Marlee swung her book satchel on top of the drink box at Harper's Store. "I wanna buy some Easter candy for you to take, okay, Caleb?" She and Alice went inside, ringing the brass bell when they opened the door.

"Let's get a drink. I'm thirsty," Albert said.

The winter showed signs of giving way to spring, and Easter break had finally arrived. The late April sun was getting hot by afternoon, and the children had stopped at Harper's for their usual snack after school.

Caleb pushed Marlee's books aside, opened the drink box, and waved to Mr. Harper, who sat behind his counter reading his newspaper. Albert dug around in the box for a Dr. Pepper while Caleb fumbled with the bottle opener on the side of the box. The boys stepped out into the warm sun and sat on a row of old tires used to border the parking area.

Albert created a little seat in the sand for his drink bottle, picked up some small pieces of gravel, and tossed them into an old tire resting a few feet away. "I still can't believe you ain't goin' fishin' with us tomorrow. I mean, it's the first and biggest trip this spring."

Caleb shrugged. "They'll be others."

"Why do you wanna go up to Cedar Hills anyway? It's just an ol' Easter egg hunt. There'll be more of *them,* too." Albert knocked his drink over and snatched it up before too much of it spilled into the sand.

"My mamma's Sunday School class is in charge of it, and I told her I'd help. Besides, I'm gonna check on Annabelle and Abigail. I haven't seen them since the night of the fire."

"Well, gosh, Marlee ain't even goin'. I don't see why you hav' to." Albert tossed a rock out of disgust more than aim. "You tryin' for another medal or somethin'?"

"No!" Caleb jerked his head angrily at Albert. "I didn't even want the one I got."

"I don't get it. I mean, th' town has a big ceremony, and the mayor gives you a medal for bein' a hero, or somethin', and you don't even wear it. All you do is keep it in your underwear drawer wrapped in that ol' handkerchief. Shoot, I'd be wearin' it to bed!"

Caleb looked at the ground. "I wasn't no hero."

"That's not the way I heard the story. You even had your picture in the newspaper!"

"Well, I wasn't the only one, then."

"I know. But some of the firemen got accom...accom..."

"Commendations," Caleb interrupted. "But I wasn't talkin' about them."

"You can't go givin' medals to some mangy ole hound dogs." Albert laughed and tossed another rock.

"It was Smoky who helped us all. I've told you that a hundred million times." Caleb grimaced and hurled a rock at the stop sign.

"Well then, you can't go givin' medals to dead men either."

They heard the door jingle when Marlee and Alice left the store.

"I've got some neat candy bunnies for Annabelle

and Abigail. I wish I could go, but my mamma's making me go shopping for my Easter dress." Marlee pinched the side of her skirt and sashayed a couple of steps. Caleb lowered his head and kicked a puff of dust from the gravel parking lot.

"These are *so* good!" Alice said, licking pink icing from the corner of her mouth. "And they're only three for a nickel!"

"I'm gonna get me some!" Albert was already digging into his pocket for coins.

"I need to get home. Here, how 'bout paying for my drink when you go in, okay?" Caleb placed his empty bottle into the wire rack by the box and handed Albert a dime.

"Sure. See you Sunday. Hope the Easter bunny comes to see ya!" Albert and Alice disappeared into the store.

"Whatcha doing during Easter break?" Marlee asked as they walked along Cane Creek Road toward home.

Caleb shrugged. "I'm gonna help some down at the Services with my mama. In the mornings, anyways. Wanna come? There's lots to do there."

"Maybe. I'm not sure what I'm doing. You've been going there a lot this winter. I've barely seen you. What do you do down there?"

"Oh, there's always something need'n to be done. This winter, I mostly helped deliver firewood to folks. I'm not sure what's goin' on next week."

The two friends walked down Cane Creek Road in silence. Marlee paused at her drive and then smiled at Caleb. "Well, here's the candy for the girls. Tell Annabelle and Abigail I said hello, and hug them for me."

"I'll tell them."

They hesitated a moment, but neither spoke.

"Well, see you Sunday." Marlee turned and strolled up the drive toward her house.

Caleb stood and watched her walk away from him before turning toward home.

****

Caleb stepped from the door of the old yellow bus onto the church parking lot. He had loaded the last of the Easter baskets for the children at Cedar Hills. He stood, picking green cellophane grass from his shirt sleeve, when his mother walked up beside him.

"Caleb, you've done so much to help. Why don't you go fishing with the fellas? You could catch up to them if you hurried."

He looked at the cloudless, blue sky, and in his mind, he saw the sunlight dancing across the water when his float plopped into the lake after a perfect cast. Temptation almost pulled him home to collect his fishing gear. However, something tightened deep inside, that gut feeling telling him he had more important things to do.

"No, Mama. I want to go to the Children's home. It'll be fun. Mainly, I want to see Annabelle and Abigail."

His mother beamed a proud smile. "Well then, let's get this show on the road!"

****

After they arrived at Cedar Hills Children's Home and the baskets had all been unloaded, Caleb asked Mrs. Williams if he could see Annabelle and Abigail. She led him into the parlor, where he waited while she went to get the girls.

The room was about the size of his grandparents' parlor. Everything seemed to be from another time. A large painting of a woman in a long dress playing the piano hung on one end of the room, and ivory-globed lamps with pink flowers painted on them decorated the tops of several polished end tables. The wall-to-wall carpeting had square paths left behind by a recent vacuuming. He would have preferred to lie on the rug rather than sit on the high-backed sofa, but he knew that wasn't proper behavior.

After a short wait, Mrs. Williams appeared under the archway entrance, holding Annabelle and Abigail by the hand. Caleb stared. He wouldn't have recognized them. Their long brown hair was clean and shiny, with pink bows tied in the back. Their dresses were alike, except Annabelle's was white and her sister's yellow. They both wore shiny black baby-doll shoes with frilly socks. Abigail held a doll close to her chest.

"Girls, Caleb Austin has come from the Fletcher Baptist Church and wants to visit with you for a bit." She led them into the middle of the room. Caleb stood up, not sure what to do with his hands. "We'll be out on the lawn getting ready for the egg hunt when y'all want to come out," she said, looking at Caleb. "Will you bring the girls with you?"

"Yes, Ma'am. Thanks." Caleb watched Mrs. Williams leave before speaking.

"Hi. I guess you remember me…from the fire and all." Caleb hadn't rehearsed what he had planned to say, and now he felt at a loss for words.

"I 'member ya." Annabelle stood, looking at Caleb, expressionless.

Abigail held the doll to her chest and stared at

Caleb's and Annabelle's faces.

"Um…well…you probably remember Marlee, too. She couldn't come today but sent y'all some candy." Caleb handed each girl a small brown paper sack. Abigail laid her doll gently on the sofa and unrolled the sack.

Annabelle reached in and pulled out one of the candy bunnies. She smelled it and smiled. "Thank ye."

Caleb looked at his feet and scratched a few lines in the carpet with the toe of his shoe. He wasn't sure how to approach the next subject. He was tempted to forget it, but he knew he couldn't. It was the main reason he had come.

"And, Annabelle," Caleb paused and looked at the girl. Now he knew what Marlee had meant about Annabelle's blue eyes. He felt like she already knew what he was going to say and was simply waiting. "Uh…all these people have been saying that I'm some kinda hero or somethin' because of what all happened durin' the fire, and all. Well, I think you were pretty brave yourself. I mean, you helped get Marlee outta there."

Annabelle continued to look at Caleb.

"And Smo—I mean your daddy—was the biggest hero. If it hadn't been for him, we all might have…not gotten out." Caleb reached into his pocket and pulled out Smoky's old bandanna. He carefully unfolded the cloth and held out the medallion he had received from the mayor for bravery. The bronze medal was about the size of a half-dollar and was attached to a red, white, and blue neck ribbon.

"I'm sorry about your daddy. He deserves this medal the most for bein' brave that night. I want you to have it." Caleb held it out to Annabelle and hesitated, unsure how she would react. With Caleb still holding the medal, Annabelle reached and traced the symbols and inscription, *Semper Fortis*.

"Those words are in Latin. They mean 'Always Brave.'" Then, Caleb leaned forward and placed it gently around her neck.

Annabelle held the medal lightly in her hand as if it were made of glass.

"Oh, and Abigail. This bandanna was your daddy's. It's what saved us in the fire. It kept the smoke out. I want you to have it." Caleb carefully folded the cloth and handed it to the little girl. He wasn't sure if she understood, but he knew her sister would explain it later.

Abigail touched the old red fabric to her cheek. She smiled and then scampered to the couch, unwrapped the bandanna, and swaddled her doll tightly with the cloth.

From outside, excited children shouted and cheered. Caleb turned to the window and saw boys and girls spread across the lawn, carrying colorful baskets and searching for Easter eggs. "Hey, y'all ready to hide some eggs?"

****

The next morning came a little too early for Caleb's taste.

"Time to hit the floor." Caleb's dad stuck his head through the doorway and clicked on the light switch. It was still dark outside. Caleb held his arms over his forehead and squinted from the light. Was it time for school already? He sat up in his bed and rubbed his eyes. Then he remembered. It was Easter Sunday, and they were going to the sunrise service at the cemetery. Caleb's body flopped back onto the mattress like a wet sack of sand. Why couldn't he meet them later at Sunday School?

As he walked down the porch steps, the cool April air met Caleb in an unexpected rush. He loosened his tie and took a deep breath. Caleb loved mornings; it was his body that didn't care much for them. On a few rare occasions, he had been up before the sun and watched it rise as he trotted along the road and across the field toward his grandparents' house. But today seemed like such a waste of a good spring morning to stand in a cemetery with a suit on and listen to the preacher.

Caleb's dad parked their car next to a curb, and the Pattersons' car parked a short way up the road. The county cemetery looked like an endless sea of tombstones cresting over a well-mowed knoll. The white markers reflected an eerie glow in the pre-dawn haze.

A few months back, at Smoky's funeral, some of the men at church had taken up money for his burial and tombstone, and Caleb's daddy had been asked to be a pallbearer. Preacher Anders had spoken at the service. Caleb hadn't been to the cemetery since the funeral.

Caleb walked with his parents across the grass to a level spot beside a pond. He looked around at the handful of people who gathered for the sunrise service. He didn't see Marlee. Maybe she was lucky enough to stay in bed.

He looked over his shoulder to the stand of trees where Smoky was buried with his father and brother. Caleb left his parents and strolled up the hill to the family plot. The grass was beginning to grow on the dirt covering Smoky's grave. His stone simply read *Charles Pruitt. Husband and Father. May he rest in peace.* Caleb bent down and pushed the dry weeds away from Smoky's brother's stone. The inscription read *A hero who saved many lives.*

Caleb stepped back and spoke his thoughts out loud. "But Smoky was a hero, too. If he hadn't come off the mountain and helped us, there would be a lot more tombstones out here today."

"I thought I'd find you here."

Startled, Caleb spun around to face Marlee. His breath quickened. She was beautiful in her new Easter dress. She was holding a small bouquet. "I brought these to put on Smoky's grave."

Without a word, Caleb took them from Marlee and placed the flowers in front of Smoky's headstone.

The two friends stood shoulder to shoulder in the pre-dawn light.

"He was an outcast and misunderstood..." Reverend Anders's words floated through the morning air. "As it says in the Holy Word, the gospel of Mark chapter twenty-eight:

And Jesus cried in a loud voice and gave up the ghost. And the veil of the temple was rent in twain from the top to the bottom. And when the centurion, which stood over against him, saw that he so cried out and gave up the ghost, he said, truly this man was the Son of God. Amen."

A small flock of mallards returned from an early flight and skidded across the pond, flapping and celebrating the daybreak.

As the preacher's "Amen" echoed throughout the small crowd, the sun peeked over the ridge. Caleb and Marlee stood together and watched the sunrise. The scalloped clouds slowly shifted their hues, replacing orange and pink with white, and the royal sky yielded to the lighter blue of morning.

A word about the author...

Curt Richards was raised in the upstate of South Carolina in the 1960's where his interest in nature was piqued by days exploring the forest and ponds near his home. This interest led him to Clemson University where he studied Animal Agriculture, wildlife biology, and education. After college, he became a high school Biology teacher for twenty-eight years followed by instructing anatomy at a small college for twelve years.

Richards has always had a passion for writing, especially stories steeped in the mountains and foothills of the Carolinas where he calls home.

www.curtrichards.com